DEADLY
UNNA?

PHILLIP GWYNNE

PENGUIN BOOKS

Penguin Books Australia Ltd
487 Maroondah Highway, PO Box 257
Ringwood, Victoria 3134, Australia
Penguin Books Ltd
Harmondsworth, Middlesex, England
Penguin Putnam Inc.
375 Hudson Street, New York, New York 10014, USA
Penguin Books Canada Limited
10 Alcorn Avenue, Toronto, Ontario, Canada M4V 3B2
Penguin Books (N.Z.) Ltd
Cnr Rosedale and Airborne Roads, Albany, New Zealand
Penguin Books (South Africa) (Pty) Ltd
24 Sturdee Avenue, Rosebank, Johannesburg 2196, South Africa
Penguin Books India (P) Ltd
11, Community Centre, Panchsheel Park, New Delhi 110 017, India

First published by Penguin Books, 1998
11 13 15 14 12
Copyright © Phillip Gwynne, 1998

Design by Ellie Exarchos, Penguin Design Studio
Typeset in 11.5/15 Weiss by Midland Typesetters, Maryborough, Victoria
Printed and bound in Australia by McPherson's Printing Group, Maryborough,
Victoria

National Library of Australia
Cataloguing-in-Publication data:

Gwynne, Phillip
Deadly, Unna?

ISBN 0 14 130049 3.

I. Title
A823.3

Penguin Books website: www.penguin.com.au
You can write to the author at: pgwynne@iaa.com.au

To my mum, Gaynor

WINTER

1

We've made the grand final.

Next Saturday we play Wangaroo for the Peninsula Junior Colts Premiership. The whole town is talking about it, it's the biggest thing to happen here since the second prize in the S.A. Tidy Towns Competition (Section B). Just shows what sort of town I live in. Hopeless.

Our coach, Mr Robertson, runs one of the two local stores. I call him 'Arks', behind his back of course, because he says 'arks' instead of asks and 'arksed' instead of asked.

'If I've arksed youse boys once I've arksed youse a thousand times, don't buggerise with the bloody ball on them flanks, kick the bugger up the bloody centre.'

Arks's son, Mark, is the captain of our team. He also says 'arks'. Mark has two sisters; both of them say 'arks'. It's definitely in the family, this 'arks' thing. Arks's shop is the quieter of the two, it doesn't have much of a turnover, and the Pollywaffles are always stale. I buy mine there though, just on the off-chance I can entice one of the Robertson family into saying 'arks'. It always gives me a thrill.

We've made the grand final and I'm the second ruck. First ruck is Carol Cockatoo. He's from the Point, an Aboriginal mission just up the coast. Carol is the best footballer in our side, probably on the peninsula. He's about the same size as a wheat silo. He also has quite a lot of facial hair – unusual in a fourteen year old. Once, during training, I asked him why he had a girl's name. He punched me. I never asked again.

The ruck's job is to follow the ball. When the first ruck gets tired, it's the second ruck's turn. Carol never got tired. Never. Even when the game was over he'd still be going – kicking the ball and chasing it, kicking and chasing. Often he'd be eating a pastie at the same time, a trail of tomato sauce dribbling behind. So I never did any rucking. I just hung around the forward line and hoped my mate Dumby Red would pass the ball to me so I could have a shot for goal. If you kicked a goal you got your name in the *Peninsula Gazette* on Thursday.

Half of our team is Aboriginal, boys from the mission. We call them Nungas, it's what they call them-selves as well. They're the Nungas and we're the

4

Goonyas. We're the only town on the peninsula with Nungas in our team. Without them we wouldn't be in the grand final, without them we wouldn't even have a team. They're incredibly skilful, but they infuriate Arks. He's all for directness, for going down the guts, for grabbing the ball and booting it as hard as you can. The Nungas, they just love to buggerise around on them flanks.

It's like they're playing another game, with completely different rules. The aim is not to put the ball through the big white sticks, not to score the most goals, but to keep possession, to make your opponents, and your team-mates, look slow and cumbersome. They zigzag the ball across the field, they kick it backwards, they handball it over their heads, they go on wild, bouncing runs. When the Nungas played like this, by their rules, we just stopped and watched. They never gave the ball to us – we weren't part of it, we didn't understand. Arks would be bellowing from the boundary line, his face getting redder and redder, 'Stop buggerising around and boot the bloody thing. Boot the bloody thing. For Chrissakes boot it!'

Eventually, when they finished buggerising around, when Arks's face was so red you could see it glowing like a tail-light from the other side of the field, they'd pass the ball to one of us Goonyas, usually right in front of the goals, so we couldn't miss.

Disaster! Four days before the grand final. Some snoop from Wangaroo has been out at the Point, poking about in the birth register. Carol Cockatoo is actually Colin Cockatoo, Carol's eighteen-year-old brother. Arks is devastated. He drove out to the Point to find the real Carol Cockatoo. He was short and fat and hopeless. Arks has no choice. The team has no choice. The town has no choice. I'm the only other tall player: I've got to be first ruck.

The news spreads like diesel on water. A footy game is won and lost in the ruck. Everybody knows this. It's one of the facts of life. Suddenly I'm the most important person in the town.

'How's that knee, Blacky?'

People who had previously barely acknowledged my existence were now asking intimate questions about my bodily parts.

'Groin holding up, is it big fella?'

Somebody even risked a first name.

'Ankle okay, Tim?' Tim's my brother. I've got three others, besides him, and three sisters as well. Usually people just call us Blacky. You can't blame them.

'It's Gary, and ankle's fine thanks.'

'Sure it is, just go out and wallop 'em, Blacky.'

2

Wangaroo is a one-man team. That man is the Thumper (another one of my nicknames), and he really is a man, even though he's only my age. He's the same size as Colin (who used to be Carol). When we played Wangaroo, the two of them would cancel each other out – like King Kong versus Godzilla. The umpy would bounce the ball, Godzilla would come thundering in from one side, King Kong from the other, there'd be an almighty collision, and the footy would end up on the ground. But now Colin (who used to be Carol) isn't playing. Without King Kong, Godzilla's gunna run amok. God help us.

Arks drove up to Wangaroo, to check out their birth register. Hard to believe, but the Thumper really is only fourteen. Apparently his old man dragged him out of school when he was twelve. He decided his son had a big future in the family business. The Thumper's been digging graves ever since.

You have to feel sorry for Arks. The Thumper plays footy exactly the way Arks thinks it should be played. He never goes anywhere near the flanks. Straight down the guts every single time he gets the ball. The perfect footballer, except for one small problem – he plays for them, Wangaroo, the opposition.

I reckon Arks even thought about moving to Wangaroo, just so he could be the Thumper's coach. But he's a terrible businessman. He only survives because the Nungas buy their supplies from him. And the Nungas only buy their supplies from him because he's the coach of the footy team. Arks has been the coach for ages, ever since I can remember. Nobody else really wants the job, except perhaps Porky Fraser, but he can't get to training on time, on account of his pigs.

All the kids in town, like Dazza and Pickles, hate school. Useless. Don't learn nothing. Can't wait to leave. Not me, I like school. Some of the stuff they teach is really useful. Of course the teachers try to make it useless, by using stupid examples that have nothing at all to do with the real world. But you can't take too much notice of them. Take the Thumper for example. What is it that makes him so scary? Momentum, that's what.

Momentum = Mass × Velocity.

Momentum equals mass times velocity. If you multiply the Thumper's mass (approximately one wheat

8

silo) by his velocity (considerable once he gets going) then you get his momentum – awesome.

There's no stopping a momentum like that, not if you've got the mass of a stick insect like me. I worked it out on my calculator. To equal the Thumper's momentum, to stop him once he got going, I'd have to travel at 1.47 times the speed of light. At the last school sports carnival I did the 100 metres in 18.4 seconds. That's 0.00000012 times the speed of light. See what I mean? It's hopeless.

You've got to look like you're trying to stop him, though. If you don't then you're a gutless wonder. A gutless wonder is about the worst thing you can be in our town. If you're a boy that is. If you're a girl then it's a slack moll. Slack boys, gutless girls – nobody cares. Once you've been labelled a gutless wonder, then that's it, the label sticks. Like it's been superglued to your forehead. It's there for life, no matter what you do.

I'm down at the beach. Twelve kiddies are splashing about in the shallows. Then I see it – a huge grey fin slicing through the water. I dive in, knife clenched in my teeth, and reach the shark just as it's about to make a snack of little Annie Ashburner. I wrestle, Tarzan-style, with the kid-eating monster. The water turns red with blood. The shark dies. Unfortunately, so do I. I'm dead, but a hero. I've saved twelve little lives, the future Year One of Port Primary School.

At my funeral, one father whispers to another, 'Gutsy effort, eh? Saved all those kids.'

'S'pose,' the other replies. 'But remember the day he

didn't tackle the Thumper and they kicked that goal right on the siren and we lost the grand final by the barest of margins?'

'Christ, that's right. I'd forgotten all about that. What a gutless bloody wonder, eh?'

'Too right,' says the other.

If I tackle the Thumper I'm gunna get clobbered. If I don't I'll end up with 'Gutless Wonder' superglued to my forehead. There is, however, a way out. It's called the Thumper tackle. It's my invention. What you do is launch yourself at a point just behind the galloping Thumper. Then at the last moment you desperately fling out your hand. From the boundary this looks like a legitimate tackle, but the risk to your personal well-being is minimal. You're not gutless. Hopeless, but not gutless. Your reputation survives. Your forehead remains label-free.

You can't beat the Thumper once he gets the ball. No use even trying. The idea, therefore, is to not let him get the ball. Personally, I wouldn't even let him on the ground. I'd done some research – the Thumper always ate three meat pies before a game. With sauce. I wanted to sneak into the canteen and put Ratsak in his pies. Not a lot – I didn't want to kill him. It was only a game of footy after all. Just enough to slow him down a bit. I told Arks my plan. He thought it was a great joke.

'Blacky,' he said, 'you're a funny lad.'

I wasn't joking.

3

They reckon Arks was a real champ in his day, the best footballer ever to come out of the Port. He was playing A Grade when he was only fourteen. Then some talent scout from town found him and he ended up down at Norwood, playing for the mighty Redlegs.

There's a photo of him on the wall in the pub. His hair is black and glossy, slicked back and parted in the middle. He's looking straight at the camera, square chin tilted forward, not smiling. His arms are folded against his chest. Beneath a pair of those old-fashioned baggy shorts are muscly legs, slightly bandy. *Donald B. Robertson. 232 games. Runner-Up 1962 Magarey Medal. 1964 All Australian* is written underneath.

All Australian. Runner-up in the Magarey. Arks must have been some footballer. I often wondered why he came back to the Port. Then one day I heard them talking in the front bar.

'Great player in his day, Robbo.'

'So I've heard.'

'My oath he was. But he was getting on a bit, and they offered him a fair whack to come down here as captain-coach. In them days, there was still some money around. We had a bloody good team.'

'You don't say.'

'Robbo did well too, always got 'em into the final. For some reason, and for the life of me I don't know why, they never pulled it off. They got close, bloody close, but they never won the big one. When Robbo did his knees, he hung up his boots. 'Bout that time the arse dropped outta the wheat market, money wasn't there no more. Couldn't pay no more coaches.'

'Is that right?'

'So he bought the deli. Not long after the missus shoots through. Adelaide girl, good sort too, but she never took much of a liking to sitting behind a shop counter all day. Took off with the Amscol man, leaves poor Robbo with the kids.'

'Well I'll be.'

Arks hasn't changed that much since they took that photo. A lot of footballers blow up like balloons once they stop playing. Not Arks though. He's put on a bit of weight, but not much. His hair is grey at the sides now, but he still slicks it back. Arks doesn't mind the old Brylcreem. But I suppose he gets it wholesale, because of the shop.

On Wednesday night he rang me at home. Said he wanted to pick me up at the bus stop after school so we could go up the oval and have some rucking practice.

'Isn't it a bit late for that?' I said.

'Never too late, lad. Never too late.'

'I'm not sure, Mr Robertson. Maybe I should ask my mum.'

'Already arksed her. She said it's fine. I'll see you there.'

And then he hung up.

4

'Wanna come down the jetty?' asked Pickles as we got off the bus.

'Nah, Arks is gunna pick me up. We're going up the oval. He wants to give me some tips about rucking.'

'You're joking, bit late for that isn't it?'

'That's what I was trying to tell him.'

Then came the unmistakable sound of the Arksmobile, the exhaust making huge farting noises.

'That'd be him, then,' said Pickles. 'See ya round.'

'Yeah, see ya,' I said as he walked away.

I could see the Arksmobile now, coming up the main street, a cloud of thick black smoke following behind. It pulled up next to me.

Our town was full of old utes, but the Arksmobile was something special. Full of rust and not a straight panel on it. It only passed rego because Deano Davies plays on our side (Deano's old man is the local copper).

'Gidday,' said Arks as he leant over and pushed the door open. There was no handle on the outside.

'Gidday Mr Robertson,' I said as I sat down. Inside it smelt like Brylcreem.

Arks dropped the clutch and we skidded off.

He didn't say anything as we drove back down the main street. Then suddenly –

'How ya been?'

'Pretty good.'

'Not nervous?'

'Just a bit.'

'Christ, I used to get so nervous I'd be spewing me guts out. One game there, reckon it must've been the '63 final 'gainst the Bays, I was still spewin' when we run on.'

'Geez. What was that like?'

'Spewin' me guts out?'

'Nuh, playing in a grand final in Adelaide.'

'What was it like? Can you imagine running onto the field with fifty thousand people yelling and screaming at ya?'

I tried to imagine but it didn't seem to work.

'Not really,' I said.

Arks gave me a funny look.

'Crikey, Blacky. It's just impossible to describe.'

'What about when ya won?' I said. 'What was that like?'

We turned off into the oval, and stopped behind the

goal posts. There was nobody else around. Arks turned the engine off.

'Got done. Been in eight grand finals – three in town, two here in the Port as a player and three as a coach and I never won, not one of the buggers, not a bloody one.'

Silence, just the ticking of the engine. I knew what Arks was waiting for. I was supposed to say, 'This'll be the first one, then.' Football breeds optimism like Pickles Mickle's groin breeds the munga. Three-quarter-time, your team's losing by a hundred goals, and some idiot's bound to say, 'Come on fellas, let's get out there and murder 'em.' Yeah, sure. But before you know it the whole team's getting excited, getting all optimistic.

Arks opened his door. I said nothing.

'This'll be the first one, then,' he said.

I wasn't much of a footballer. Not much of an optimist either.

The oval is on the edge of town, close to the Kapoona road, a stone's throw from Porky Fraser's pigsties. When there was an easterly blowing, like tonight, you wished they'd thrown that stone a bit further.

First we had some goal-kicking practice. I was the worst kick in our side, probably on the whole peninsula. I knew all the theory – weight evenly balanced, eyes on the ball, leg straight, toe pointed, follow right through. If they had an exam, sat you in a classroom and asked you a whole lot of questions about how to kick a footy, then I'd come top. But all this info in my head didn't get to the rest of my body. Something happened to it in transit, it got confused, muddled up. Instead of a perfect lace-out drop-punt the ball would dribble along the ground, skew off to the side, or sometimes it didn't go anywhere, I'd miss it completely. What really annoyed me was that somebody like Mark Arks, who could really boot the ball, knew bugger-all about the theory.

'Geez, I dunno, mate,' he'd say, shaking his head, if you asked him any sort of technical question.

A couple of weeks ago we were playing Murraculka. I was lining up to take a shot for goal. Dead in front. Some moron yelled out from the boundary.

'Jesus Christ, not him, he couldn't kick the ball over a jam jar.'

Of course everybody thinks this is a great joke. Even my team-mates. I missed the goal. Out on the full. After that they called me Jam-Jar Black. Only for about a week, though. It seems like the only nicknames that ever lasted were the ones I made up.

Arks stood in the goal square and I took shots at the goals. After a while he got sick of chasing after the ball.

'Okay,' he said, 'let's try some ruck work.'

In the old days all the ruck ever did was jump up and punch the ball as hard as he could. But that all changed. It was the Aboriginal champion 'Polly' Farmer who changed it. He revolutionised ruck work. He introduced skill and finesse. Instead of just punching the footy, he tapped it, he palmed it, he placed it. He thought about what he was going to do with it.

Arks threw the ball up in the air.

'Jump, lad,' he yelled, 'and thump the bloody thing.'

I jumped and I thumped. But I missed, ending up flat on my backside. A galah in the gum tree behind us squawked. Arks threw the ball up. I jumped again. I thumped again. This time I connected with a thwack! and the ball flew towards the goals.

'That's it Blacky, that's it, lad, thump the bloody thing.'

It felt good, real good. I looked triumphantly towards the gum tree.

We should've stopped then, when my confidence was up. But Arks kept tossing the ball up in the air, again and again and again. And I kept jumping and trying to thump it. It was getting dark and in the fading light the ball became blurred and indistinct. I could hardly see it. My legs were tired and my hands were sore. I was missing all the time now. Even the galah got tired of watching. It gave a final squawk and flew off towards the town.

At last Arks called it quits. He said nothing as we bounced along the back road to my place. But I could smell his disappointment, even with all that Brylcreem. Well, I thought, I might as well get some enjoyment out of tonight. I baited the hook.

'Did Dumby Red ask you about those boots?'

'What boots? He never arksed me anythink.'

Whammo! Double banger – an 'arksed' and an 'anythink'. But it didn't give me much of a thrill. Poor Arks – with his banged-up ute, his stale Pollywaffles, his baggy shorts, his Brylcreem, his missus who shot through, all those grand finals and not a bloody one. I was feeling sorry for him. This was his big chance – the talk was that next year the Point would get organised, field its own team – and he'd lost Carol, his best player, his first ruck. All he had was me – Jam-Jar Black.

We pulled up in front of the house. It was late, they'd probably started dinner already.

'You look after yourself, lad,' said Arks as I got out.

'Sure will. See ya Saturday.'

'You bet. Take care.'

'And, Mr Robertson.'

'Yes, lad.'

'Don't worry, we're gunna win this one.'

'You betcha we will,' said Arks. But he didn't sound too convinced.

5

They used to have a team out at the Point. A good one, too. They'd won heaps of flags. But then they got kicked out of the compy for brawling. Not the players, the spectators. One of them had run onto the field and decked the ump. Broke his jaw. Since then, the Nungas had played for us.

Every year, before the season started, Arks would drive out to the Point and pick up all those players who wanted a game. Then there'd be a training session so Arks could check them all out, decide who was any good. After training he'd put a list on the notice-board. This was the squad. If you weren't on that list, then bad luck pal, you had no chance of making the team.

That's when I first met Dumby Red. Arks had just been out to the Point and the Arksmobile was packed with Nungas. I knew a couple of them from last year, but the rest were strangers. Maybe I'd seen them around, but I didn't know them.

Even though the Point was only half an hour's drive from the Port, the two towns didn't have much to do with one another. The footy was really the only place where Nungas and Goonyas got to hang around together.

There must've been about forty of us in the change rooms. Usually, especially at the start of the season, the Nungas got changed at one end and us Goonyas at the other. There was no rule or anything, it was just the way it was.

I was sitting down, lacing up my boots. The place next to me was empty. I'd bagsed it for Pickles. We always sat together.

Mark Arks was parading around in his jockstrap. He was the only one in our team who had one, the rest of us just wore our undies. A jockstrap, in case you don't know, is a weird-looking contraption that's supposed to offer extra protection to the reproductive organs. Mark Arks thought that because he had a jockstrap there was something special about his reproductive organs. But I'd seen them a few times and they looked pretty ordinary to me.

Somebody sat down next to me.

'That's Pickles' spot,' I said without looking up.

'All look the same to me, brudda,' came the reply.

I sat up. It was a Nunga, one I didn't know. He was smiling. I couldn't help noticing his teeth. They were perfect. He wasn't tall, but not short either. Slim,

athletic-looking. He had long hair, shoulder length.
And he was wearing Levi's, a denim shirt and basketball
boots with red stars on the side and red laces.

What great boots! I'd never seen any like that before.
He hadn't bought them local, that's for sure.

'Any hangers around here?' he said, undoing the
buttons on his shirt.

'You've gotta be joking,' I said.

Hangers? There weren't even proper hooks, just nails
banged into the wall.

'You play footy?' he said.

'Yeah, I'm the second ruck. What about you, what
position d'you play?'

'Dunno,' he said.

'Whatta ya mean you dunno?'

'We don't play no positions out the Point. We just
run around and dob the footy. None of that position
stuff.'

He took a jumper from his bag. It was blue – Carlton
colours. Then he pulled it on over his head. I could see
the number now. It was 25. Unbelievable! – he was
wearing Jezza's number! My hero, the best footballer on
the planet, and this dumb Nunga who didn't even know
what position he played was wearing his jumper.

'Anyways, what your name called?' he said.

'Gary. But everybody calls me Blacky. What's
yours?'

'Dumby Red.'

'What?'

'Dumby Red.'

'Why they call you that?'

'It's me name, unna.'

'But it's not your proper name, is it? It's not what's on your birth certificate?'

'I don't know nothing 'bout that birth certificate stuff, all I know is me name's Dumby Red.'

When he'd done up his boots he took out a white comb.

'There a mirror round here?' he said.

'Over there,' I said, pointing.

He walked over, and started combing his hair.

Pickles arrived.

'Whose stuff is this?' he said, annoyed.

I nodded towards Dumby. He was still combing his hair.

'Okay, let's get out there,' bellowed Arks.

The other players started to move outside. I waited for Pickles to get changed. We were the last to leave, except for Dumby. He was still at it, combing away.

'You coming?' I said.

'Yep,' he said, slipping his comb into his sock.

'Okay, lads, two laps warm-up,' said Arks.

There was a chorus of groans.

'Get to it. Now!' he said.

We took off. I was at the back with Dazza and Pickles. Dumby Red was in front of us. The pace was slow and we all kept together. Then about halfway through the second lap Arks yelled, 'Sprint it in from there.' Pickles soon dropped behind. Dazza and I had our usual race. I looked ahead expecting to see Mark

Arks in the lead. He was the school sprint champion after all. But instead it was Dumby who was first. And was doing it easy too, with long balanced strides.

'Geez, can he run, or what?' said Dazza after we'd arrived.

'Doesn't mean he can play footy,' I said. This Dumby Red kid was starting to annoy me.

'Circle work,' yelled Arks, after Pickles had struggled in last. We spread out across the oval.

Arks kicked the ball towards Dumby.

'Mark it,' he yelled.

Dumby took a couple of strides, jumped up easily, grabbed the ball in front of his eyes and stabbed it with his left foot back to Arks. It thudded into his chest.

'And again,' yelled Arks.

This time he grubbered the ball along the ground. Dumby ran straight at it, scooped it up one-handed and kicked it back. With his right foot this time. Again it thudded into Arks's chest.

After training Arks pinned the list to the notice-board. All of us crowded around. Top of the list was Mark Arks. The next name down was Dumby Red's. Further down was my name. Then Dazza's. Pickles' was last.

Arks was in a good mood, laughing and cracking jokes as the Nungas piled back into the Arksmobile. He knew he'd have a good side – Mark Arks in the centre and Carol leading the ruck. And if this Dumby Red played like he trained, then Arks'd found the forward he'd been looking for. Maybe this'd be his big chance.

Dazza, Pickles and I started walking home.

'Nukkin ya, Blacky,' yelled Dumby from the back of the Arksmobile as it rattled past.

'Nukkin ya' is Nunga talk for 'see ya'.

'Mate of yours now, is he?' said Pickles.

'No way. Not him. I hate his guts,' I said, and I spat on the ground just to show I meant it.

And I suppose I did mean it. This Dumby Red was trendy, he was talented, he was up himself, he wore Jezza's number 25, and he had that smile.

A couple of months later we were playing Tangaratta, at Tangaratta. They were a hopeless team, but they had Mad Dog. He was a scrawny kid with dirty blond hair that hung over his mean eyes and a mouth full of busted teeth. Mad Dog was a hopeless player, but that didn't matter, he never went for the ball anyway. He'd do anything to put you off your game – punch you in the stomach, elbow you in the face, kick you in the nuts. Anything.

We thrashed them 27.9 to 1.2. Dumby kicked eight goals from the half-forward flank. Eight more than me. I didn't even touch the ball. I spent the whole game making sure I was nowhere near Mad Dog.

After the game was over, a few of us – me, Mark Arks, Deano, Pickles, Dazza, and a couple of others – decided to check out the town. It didn't take long. There wasn't much to check out – just a few empty streets. The only place open was the servo.

'There's ya mate,' said Pickles.

Dumby and Clemboy, another Nunga, were coming

out of the servo. Both of them were munching on a packet of chips.

'Piss off, he's not my mate,' I said. 'I hate his guts.'

But this time I didn't spit, because I didn't mean it. A terrible thing had happened – I'd stopped hating Dumby Red's guts. I couldn't help it, I'd started to like him.

I suppose in the beginning I was jealous, because he was so talented. He could do it all, all the clichés – take the big grab, snap goals from impossible angles, kick equally well with either foot, run past people like they were standing still. He could've kicked ten goals every match if he wanted to, but he gave out heaps of handballs. If you called for the ball he'd pass it to you. He was a real team player.

Dumby was totally up himself, there's no denying that. He couldn't walk past a mirror or a shop-window without stopping. I'd even caught him looking at his reflection in a puddle, giving that white comb of his a good workout.

Despite this I still liked him. Probably because he was mad. Really mad. Madder than a cut snake. Life was never boring when he was around.

So I stopped hating Dumby's guts. Except I still acted like I did. I was used to it, I suppose. It was easier to stay like that.

'What a dump,' said Mark Arks. 'I'm going back.'

'Me, too,' said Dazza.

Everybody agreed there wasn't a lot of excitement to be had in Tangaratta.

Then we met them, a gang of Tangaratta kids coming the other way. Mad Dog was one of them. We stopped. They stopped. We looked at them. They looked at us.

'What are youse looking at?' said Pickles.

'What are youse looking at?' said a red-haired kid with heaps of freckles.

'What's it to you, bloodnut?' said Pickles.

'Nuffin,' said Bloodnut. 'What's it to you, scumbag?'

It went on like this for quite a while. Pickles and the Bloodnut exchanging compliments. Nobody seemed to be getting the better of it. I was losing interest. My stomach was desirous of a pie.

'Let's go,' I said. 'I'm hungry.'

'Yeah, let's go,' said Dazza, and we started to walk away.

Then Bloodnut yelled, 'Get 'im Mad Dog!'

Before I knew it Mad Dog had me in a headlock. I'm not sure why he chose me. Maybe it was because I was the tallest. Maybe it was because he didn't like the look of me. Maybe it was because I'd spent the whole game running away from him, and he hadn't had the chance to punch me in the stomach, elbow me in the face, or kick me in the nuts. Whatever the reason, he had his arm around my neck and my nose was wedged up against his armpit. It didn't feel good. It smelt even worse. Mad Dog was scrawny, but he sure was strong. Whenever I tried to pull my head free he'd give a mad cackle and rap me on the top of the head with his knuckles.

'Help me! Help me! Get him off me!' I screamed. Nobody, none of my team-mates, did a thing.

Then he started spinning me around and around. I was getting dizzy.

'Whatta ya reckon? Into the turnbuckle,' he said.

Into the turnbuckle was an illegal, but effective, tactic used by the wrestlers on the telly. The baddy would ram the goody's head into the turnbuckle. And even though the turnbuckle was well-padded and the wrestlers were only acting, it still looked painful.

But where, I wondered, was Mad Dog going to find a turnbuckle in the main street of Tangaratta?

When I saw what he had in mind I started to get really worried.

'Help, help, for Chrissakes help!' I yelled, as loud as I could.

Mad Dog wanted to ram my head into a Stobie pole. Stobie poles are made from steel and concrete. They don't have much padding.

'Better let him go,' said Bloodnut. 'He's shittin' himself.'

'Yeah, let him go. He's shitting himself,' everybody agreed, especially me.

Everybody except Mad Dog.

'Into the turnbuckle,' he said, and he started running.

I looked up, the Stobie pole was looming closer and closer. Just when I could feel my head crunching against the concrete, Mad Dog loosened his grip. I pulled free.

I spun around. Now Dumby Red had Mad Dog in

a headlock. And he was really squeezing, too. Mad Dog's face was getting redder and redder.

'Ya had enough?' said Dumby. 'Had enough?'

The Mad Dog was doing everything he could to get free. But he couldn't. Dumby had him in a vice-like.

'Enough,' said Mad Dog, finally. 'Enough.'

Dumby let go. Mad Dog turned around with his hand outstretched.

'No hard feelings,' said Mad Dog. 'Shake on it.'

It was the honourable way to end a fight.

'No hard feelings,' said Dumby, smiling.

As Dumby went to take his hand, Mad Dog swung his left fist around in a huge haymaker. It caught Dumby on the side of his face. His head snapped back. I thought it'd knock him out, a punch like that. Dumby wobbled a bit, but he stayed on his feet.

He was looking at Mad Dog, like he couldn't comprehend what had just happened.

'Don't shake hands with no boongs,' said Mad Dog.

The first punch landed flush on his nose. There was a crunching noise and blood spurted out. The second punch closed his eye. The third punch would've killed him I reckon, but it didn't connect. Mad Dog ducked, and took off down the street like a startled rabbit. The rest of his gang followed.

'Thanks, Dumby,' I said as we all walked back to the oval.

'That's okay,' he said, rubbing the side of his face. He let me have one of his killer smiles.

It was just the excuse I needed. Now I could stop

hating Dumby's guts. Thank God for that.

Next Thursday we were walking home from training when the Arksmobile came flying past.

'Nukkin ya, Blacky,' yelled Dumby as he leant out over the side.

'Nukkin ya, Dumby,' I yelled, almost involuntarily.

'Nukkin ya?' said Pickles. 'Geez, you're talking like one of them now.'

'So what,' I said.

'Well I s'pose he is a mate of yours and all,' said Pickles.

'Matter of fact, he is,' I said.

6

I walked into the kitchen. The whole tribe was there, sitting around the kitchen table, waiting for dinner to be served. Except for the old man, of course. As usual, he was down the pub. He only sat down to eat with us when the pub was closed – Sundays and Christmas Day.

Mum was at the stove, wooden spoon in her hand, stirring the contents of a large pot. She was wearing a checked apron.

'How was the training?' she said.

'All right I s'pose.'

'You don't sound too convinced.'

My mum loved the footy. She came to every match, and there wasn't much she didn't know about the game, especially tactics. I'm sure she would've been a better coach than Arks. I'd thought of suggesting it to him, that Mum could be appointed tactical adviser. Send somebody over at the end of each quarter to get her thoughts. Or maybe they could use walkie-talkies. But I knew Arks wouldn't have a bar of it. Everybody thought that to be a great coach you had to have been a great player. And a bloke, of course. They weren't going to listen to somebody's roly-poly mum, even if she was a tactical genius. No way.

'I don't know what Arks, I mean Mr Robertson, expects of me.'

'That you do your best. That's all anybody expects. Do your best and he'll be as happy as Larry.'

This was one of my mum's sayings – as happy as Larry. She said it all the time. But I didn't understand it. Who was Larry? Why was he happy? And how happy was he actually? Now, if she said as happy as a pig in mud, then that was a different thing. I'd been out to Porky Fraser's pigsties, I'd seen a pig in mud, I'd seen the smile on that pig's face. I could tell that it was an extremely happy pig. But Larry?

I sat down. The chair wobbled. It was the one with the wonky leg. Last to sit down always got it.

'Good evening, erstwhile siblings,' I said.

'Sibling' was one of my favourite words. I discovered it last year, when I'd helped Mum fill in the census form. Now I used it all the time. 'Erstwhile' I got at the doctor's surgery. It was in a *Reader's Digest* – 'Increase Your Word Power'.

Nobody answered. The erstwhile siblings were all a bit fed-up with my increased word power.

The table had been neatly set. I knew Sharon had done it, because she did everything neatly. Her hair was always combed, her room, or her part of the room, was always tidy. I felt sorry for her, a neat person like her in a great big messy family like ours.

The tablecloth (plastic, with pictures of sailing boats) hung evenly over the table's edges. The plates and cutlery were neatly laid out. Salt and pepper shakers, a plate piled high with sliced white bread, and a plastic tub of marg in the middle.

It was neat, but none of the stuff matched. A few plates were from the same set, the rest were completely different. Same with the knives, the forks and the spoons. I never really paid much attention to this until I went to Adelaide for a footy carnival and stayed with this posh family called the Simcocks. In their house everything matched. It was incredible. After that I couldn't help noticing.

'I seen you up the oval, Gary,' said Kevin. 'Trying to kick the footy.'

'Saw, not seen,' said Mum from the stove. 'I saw you up the oval.'

Mum was really tough on stuff like that. She'd pounce on it like a cat on a mouse.

'But Dad talks like that,' said Kevin.

He was right there. The old man'd say things like, 'We seen him down the pub' or 'I done it yesterday'.

'I don't care how your father talks,' said Mum, 'I don't want you talking like that.'

Mum always spoke properly, and she hardly ever

swore. Actually she sounded quite posh, especially when she was on the phone, or when somebody like Mrs Ashburner came to visit. Pickles reckoned my mum had a touch of the Mary Poppins about her.

'Okay,' said Kevin. 'I saw you up the oval trying to kick the footy.'

But there's no way I wanted to talk about me up the oval trying to kick the footy. I tried a diversionary tactic.

'We'll be watching "Gilligan's Island" tonight, then,' I said.

'No way! Gilligan sucks,' said Jenny.

'"The Brady Bunch" sucks even more,' said Kevin.

It worked. It always did. My family's favourite argument — 'Gilligan's Island' versus 'The Brady Bunch'.

'Brady Bunch makes me wanna vomit,' said Claire.

'Gilligan makes me vomit,' said Jenny.

'Me too. How long's he been stuck on that stupid island, anyway?' said Best Team-man.

'Doesn't matter. Brady Bunch are total losers,' said Sharon.

'The skipper's a moron,' said Kevin.

'Marsha's a moll,' said Chris.

It always amazed me how my own siblings could argue so much about such a thing. The three little ones were just little kids, they didn't know any better. But the others had no excuse. It was so obvious, anybody with half a brain could see that there was no compari-son. 'Gilligan's Island' was the best thing on telly and 'The Brady Bunch' was just too stupid for words.

'Okay then, let's vote.'

'Yeah, let's vote.'

Us Blacks had a special way of voting. None of this one person, one vote nonsense. Whoever came up with that obviously didn't have their thinking cap on straight. We added up ages.

'All those for "The Brady Bunch",' said Best Team-man.

The Brady Bunchers put their hands up.

'My fifteen plus Jenny's twelve equals twenty-seven, plus ten for Kev equals thirty-seven, plus six for Greggy equals forty-three. Forty-three for "The Brady Bunch",' announced Best Team-man triumphantly.

It didn't look good. One of the dastardly Brady Bunchers must have bribed Greggy because usually he voted for Gilligan. It didn't take too much, a Tim-Tam would do the trick.

'All those for "Gilligan's Island".'

The Gilligan's Islanders put their hands up. I added up the ages.

'My fourteen plus thirteen for Shaz equals twenty-eight, plus Chris's eight equals thirty-six, plus Claire's eight equals forty-four. Forty-four for "Gilligan's Island". "Gilligan's Island" wins!'

'You cheated!' yelled Best Team-man. 'Fourteen plus thirteen's twenty-seven, not twenty-eight. And Claire's seven, not eight. That makes forty-two. We win.'

'Just testing,' I said.

Even though we'd lost I still reckoned our system was great. I've got nothing against little kids, but let's face it, they don't know much, do they? That's why they're always pestering you with crazy questions. The older you get, the more you know. And because you know more, you should have more say, your voting power should be greater. I was going to write to the Prime Minister to tell him about the Black system of voting, but it was so obvious, I'm sure he already knew all about it.

'Dinner's ready,' said Mum.

She served it out – chops, mashed spud and peas. Then she made herself a cup of Nescafé (black, one sugar), lit a ciggie, and sat down on a stool to do the crossword.

'What's for sweets, Mum?' said Claire when we'd finished.

'Bread and butter pudding.'

The siblings groaned. Not one of us liked bread and butter pudding. And that's why Mum made it all the time. She knew that if she served it up on Monday it'd still be there on Friday. Then we'd start eating it (reluctantly), because we knew there wouldn't be any other sweets, not until we polished off that horrible bread and butter pudding.

It was still only Thursday. Nobody wanted any sweets.

'No takers?' said Mum. 'Let's get these dishes done then.'

It didn't take long to do the dishes, it never did, not with the eight of us. By the time we'd finished,

'Gilligan's Island' was just about to start. Except tonight the Brady Bunchers had won. I went to my bedroom instead.

Except it wasn't really my bedroom, it was our bedroom, because all us boys were in one room. All the girls in the other.

There were three double bunks. Kevin and I shared one of them. I was on the top. Greggy and Chris shared another. Best Team-man had one to himself, on account of his socks. He had the smelliest feet in the Southern Hemisphere. Even Pickles was jealous of Team-man's feet. It was strange – we had the same mother, the same father, we ate the same food, we lived in the same house, we slept in the same bedroom and we used the same soap, yet my feet didn't smell at all. Honest. Obviously Team-man inherited the stinky feet gene. Not from our parents, though. The old man had weird feet, but they didn't stink. Neither did Mum's.

But that's genetics for you. Some nasty little gene, like the stinky feet gene, hiding out in its chromosome, generation after generation, waiting for the right opportunity, for the right victim. Then watch out, here it comes.

'Hi everybody, I'm the stinky feet gene.'

So you really couldn't blame Team-man. Still, none of us were keen on sleeping in the same room as him, let alone the same bunk.

The room was a mess. Even when it was tidy it was a mess. But tonight it wasn't even a tidy mess. There was stuff strewn all over the floor – undies, footy shorts, footy socks, school jumpers, snorkelling gear, magazines, bike parts.

I made my way to my bunk, and lay down. Focus on your opponent, Arks had said. Think about his strengths. His weaknesses. I closed my eyes and started zooming in on the Thumper. His weaknesses? He didn't have any! Except maybe that he wasn't too bright. But on the footy field that's not really a weakness, more like a strength. His strengths? It was too scary. I opened my eyes.

Right above me was the scar. When we first moved to the Port we lived in a caravan. Of course there weren't so many siblings then, only three or maybe four. Then the old man bought a house at a government auction. Got it for a song, he said. Great, except we were in the Port and the house was on the other side of the peninsula. So what does the old man do? He cuts the house in half, puts each half on the back of a truck and carts them over to the Port. Then he sticks the two halves back together. Hey presto – a house! You could still see where he cut it though – 'the scar', we called it.

The door opened.

'What ya doing?' said Team-man.

'Focusing on my opponent. Strengths and weaknesses.'

'You're gunna get murdered.'

'Thanks a lot.'

'Well, you are.'

'If I get murdered we'll lose. Game's won and lost in the ruck.'

'Probably.'

'Great team-man you are, Team-man.'

'I told you not to call me that, Bucky.'

'Are you staying here, or what?'

'Maybe.'

'I'm going then.'

'Good riddance.'

7

Best Team-man's real name is Timothy. Timothy James Black. But almost everybody called him Best Team-man, or Team-man or BT. I was proud of Best Team-man (the nickname, not the person). It'd been a great success.

Team-man was our back-pocket player. He was shorter than me, but bigger and stronger. Just the right build for a footballer, especially a back-pocket player. He had plenty of pace, he could kick with both feet, and he was a pretty good mark.

At training he starred. Kicking drills, marking drills, handballing drills, circle work – he made it all look so easy. This kid's got it all, you'd think if you saw him. Destined for greater things. Play for his state one day, he will. Bet me bottom dollar on that. Well, you'd lose that bottom dollar, Team-man was never going to play for the state. Because on the day, during the match, something happened. Rather, something didn't happen. He didn't get the ball. He didn't get anywhere near the ball. Best Team-man just never seemed to be in the right place at the right time.

It was hard to understand but it had something to do with what Arks called 'reading the game'.

'Youse have gotta read the game,' he'd say.

It sounded stupid. How can you read a game of footy? It's not a newspaper or a book. But I sort of knew what Arks meant. It was like a sixth sense, an instinct. Somebody like Dumby Red had it in buckets. He was always in the right place. It was like the ball followed him around. But when it came to reading the game, Team-man was completely dyslexic.

And it's not as if he didn't try. He did, more than anybody else. He was absolutely dedicated. He'd do anything for the team. He was like one of those lemmings who jump off cliffs so the other lemmings will have enough food to eat. Best Team-man would jump off a cliff, too. All Arks needed to do was arks.

'Gather 'round now, lads. I need one of youse to jump off that extremely large cliff over there.'

Before you knew it Team-man would be tumbling through the air about to join the mashed lemmings on the jagged rocks below.

Team-man was a hopeless player, but because he trained so hard and was so dedicated, he always won the Best Team-man trophy at the end of the year. Our

41

lounge room was full of them. Everywhere you looked – Best Team-man trophies. Little silver men looking back at you. There were four just on top of the telly.

I reckon a family is a lot like a team. Perhaps it's the original team. You'd think, wouldn't you, that given his lemming-like qualities, Team-man would be just about the best sibling you could have? Do anything for you, for the family. Good theory, but wrong.

Last summer we rowed right out to the reef, half-way to the island, in the old man's dinghy. We weren't supposed to take it that far, but it was the best place to go spear-fishing.

Team-man found two crays under a ledge. It was tricky catching crayfish. You could spear them, but you weren't supposed to, it was against the law. So the idea was to grab them with your hands and yank them out of their cubby-holes. These two crays were down pretty deep. When you're down that deep you have to equal-ise, pinch your nostrils, or pressure will build up in your ears.

I was using the spear, prodding the crays, trying to persuade them to move out of their hole, while Best Team-man was on the other side of the ledge, ready to grab one as it scuttled out. Finally one of the crays moved forward, but Team-man wasn't there to catch it. He'd gone. What an idiot!

I looked up. He was floating on the surface, arms out-stretched, face down. When I got closer I could see blood trickling from his left ear. I dragged him into the dinghy, and rowed like a maniac back to the shore.

We passed the jetty. Darcy was fishing in his usual spot, right at the end.

'Tim's got the bends!' I yelled out to him.

Darcy got his car and we got Best Team-man to Doc Matthews. He didn't have the bends of course. He'd busted his eardrum, that's all.

Later the old man asked us why we went out to the reef, when we weren't supposed to. He was pretty ropable (not unusual). Best Team-man said it was my idea, all my idea. My idea! The lying bastard. After I'd saved his miserable life.

Of course the old man believed Team-man, he always did.

Now is that the behaviour of a true lemming?

8

I walked outside. It was a clear night. No moon, and lots of stars in the sky.

What had Malcolm Prestwidge told me? That some of those stars were already dead, they no longer existed, they'd burnt themselves out. But we still saw them because they were so far away and it took ages for the light to reach us. I looked up at the Milky Way. It was hard to believe, but that Malcolm Prestwidge was as brainy as anything, and there wasn't much he didn't know about the universe.

I could see Darcy, our neighbour, sitting on his verandah.

'Gidday, Darcy,' I yelled. 'What ya up to?'

'Bottling up some gents, young'un. Why don't ya come over and give me a hand?'

'I'm on me way.'

Old Darcy was a little bloke, jockey size, with a big nose, like a beak. He always wore the same clothes, no matter what the weather – long khaki trousers, a long-sleeved khaki shirt buttoned at the wrists, and sand-shoes. We thought he was mad, dressed like that in the middle of summer when we spent all day with just our bathers on.

'The A-rabs,' Darcy would say, 'have been in the desert for centuries, and you don't see them running about half-naked.'

And sometimes, when I lay in bed, flat on my stomach, my back raw and aching from sunburn, I'd think that perhaps old Darcy wasn't so mad after all.

He always wore an old army hat with a seagull feather stuck in the band. There were hooks and swivels and lures and little coils of fishing gut as well. He was a walking tackle shop, old Darcy.

Every day, without fail, Darcy would be up the jetty, in his favourite spot – right at the end, sitting on his tackle box, a rod in his hands. He had a boat, a little runabout, and sometimes you'd see him in it, turning the motor over, pumping out the bilge. But that was it, I'd never seen it leave the moorings, and Darcy always seemed to be in a big hurry to get back onto the jetty.

'Pull up a seat,' said Darcy.

There weren't any seats, except for the old cane chair Darcy was sitting in, just a jumble of wooden fishing crates. His house was full of stuff he'd found washed up on the rocks – weird twisted pieces of wood, glass buoys, scraps of net, shells, whales' teeth, old bottles. I turned a crate on its side and sat down.

Darcy had a newspaper spread across his lap. In the middle of it, just below a photo of the Prime Minister, was a pile of squirming maggots.

'Whatta ya reckon young'un, nice lookin' batch of gents?' said Darcy.

Darcy always called maggots, 'gents'. It was the polite term.

Gents were Darcy's passion. Ever since he retired, about two hundred years ago, he'd been breeding them. He sold them to the campers – fifty for a dollar. Darcy's gents were famous – guaranteed to catch a feed of fish, or money back.

'What do the silly old buggers do when they retire?' he'd ask, and then he'd answer his own question.

'I'll tell you what they do, young'un. They grow bloody great pumpkins that you can't eat. Or they spend all day long playing bloody bingo. Or they hitch a caravan up behind and drag it round the country at thirty miles an hour clogging up the highways. Or they do a bit of concretin'. Or they breed roses. Well, young'un, I breed gents. There's no tickets on me, you know that, but I'm proud of what I do. There's plenty breeding roses, but I tell you what, there's not many of us breeding gents.'

He picked up an empty Vegemite jar from the floor, pulled the feather out of his hat, and used it to sweep the maggots, one at a time, into the open mouth of the jar. I could hear him counting under his breath – 'Forty-eight, forty-nine, fifty,' he said, and then he handed me the jar.

'Wanna put some burley in this one for me, young'un?'

'Sure,' I said. I held the jar up to the light. I'm no expert but your Darcy gent did look special – fatter and whiter than your average maggot. More squirm to them, too.

'What type of gents are these anyway?' I asked as I screwed the lid on.

If you got old Darcy talking gents, there was no stopping him. Usually I didn't encourage him too much – it wasn't my ideal topic of conversation – but tonight was different. I wanted to get the Thumper out of my head.

'That there's your fruit gent. Bred 'em on some old bananas I got from Robbo.'

Darcy had this theory – that different types of fish went for different types of gents, depending on what they were bred on.

'Your tommy ruff'll bite on that. So will your leathery. But your gar prefers the meat. And your flatty, well your flatty is a vicious bastard, he'll take just about anything. But I reckon nine times out of ten he'll bite on the pig guts.'

'Is that so?' I said, expecting Darcy to continue. He had numerous theories about maggots; this was just one of them.

But some of the remaining maggots were trying to

escape, making a run for it, across the Prime Minister's scowling face. Darcy carefully steered them back into the middle. No matter what he was doing – tying a knot, baiting a hook, landing a fish, or sweeping gents – Darcy did it slowly and precisely. I suppose this is what happens when you get old, you get into a groove, like a fishing reel.

'Lively buggers. They'll dance on the hook, they will,' he said.

'Young'un,' he said. 'Did I ever tell you about when I was in the RAAF and those chooks got on the runway?'

'Nuh, don't think I'd heard that one,' I said.

I had though. I'd heard all Darcy's yarns before. Umpteen times. But I didn't mind sitting through them again. Darcy had a way of telling a yarn – he'd chuckle, he'd shake his head in amazement, he'd repeat the punch-line at least ten times. Like he was hearing it for the first time himself.

As he told the yarn, I thought about what they said in the front bar, that Darcy hadn't been in the air force, that he'd spent his working life as some clerk at the post office. I didn't believe them, of course. If he hadn't been in the RAAF then how did he know so much about the war? Sure, he had a lot of books – I reckon he had every Biggles book that was ever written – but that wasn't enough: he must have been there, too.

'What about "Kaiser Bill"?' I said.

'Kaiser Bill' was a poem about some old German who gave everybody a hard time during the war. It always gave me a thrill to hear Darcy recite 'Kaiser Bill'. Just like when Arks said arks, or Shirl got on the turps and started one of her 'Mick, you rotten bludger' tirades. I think it was because even though Darcy swore a fair bit, he didn't use the really bad swear words, but 'Kaiser Bill' was chock full of them.

'"Kaiser Bill", eh?' said Darcy, looking over his shoulder, as if there might be somebody there. 'Crikey, you'll get me in strife one day, you will, young'un.'

He stopped sweeping maggots, and leaned forward towards me. His eyes narrowed.

> *Kaiser Bill you bastard*
> *Why did you start this war*
> *and send us all a-fighting*
> *you dirty rotten whore*

And when he came to the last verse his voice became low and conspiratorial –

> *and when you're tired of living*
> *a hopeless bloody wreck*
> *may you slip back through your arsehole*
> *and break your fucking neck*

I liked that about Darcy, he didn't say 'break your effing neck', or 'break your flippin' neck' or 'break your ruddy neck'. He said it just like they said it back then, in the trenches, or wherever they were.

Darcy tipped the maggots back out of the jar onto the paper.

'What'd you do that for?' I said.

'Lost me count.'

He started sweeping again, counting out loud. 'One,

two, three ... forty-seven, forty-eight, forty-nine. Damn! I'm one short.'

'Who's gunna know?' I said.

'They pay for fifty, they get fifty,' said Darcy emphatically. 'I'm not gunna start gypping people now, not at my age. Be right back.'

He folded the newspaper into a neat square. Then he got up, grabbed the torch that was on the table, and disappeared down the front steps. The gents lived out the back in forty-four gallon drums. He returned a couple of minutes later, his right hand cupped.

'Here he is,' he said. 'Number fifty, and a fine-looking gent he is too.'

He dropped the gent into the jar with the other forty-nine.

'You're looking a mite preoccupied tonight, young'un. Not your usual self. Got something or another on your mind?'

'The footy,' I said.

'The footy. I thought so,' said Darcy.

He didn't really follow the footy, he was too busy fishing and breeding gents. But he knew we were in the grand final. The whole peninsula knew that.

'They disqualified Carol. So I'm the first ruck now,' I said.

'A lot of responsibility, eh?'

That word again – responsibility. I'd been hearing it so much lately. From my teachers, from my parents, from everybody. Because I was tall (was that my fault?) and I played footy (what else was there to do in the

50

Port?) and we made the grand final (blame Dumby Red for that – he's the one who kicked the goal that got us through) and Carol gets disqualified (not by me) and the game is won and lost in the ruck (a fact of life), I ended up with all this responsibility. It didn't seem fair. It wasn't fair.

'Too much.'

'Well, young'un. All I can say is, do your best.'

Do your best. That's what Mum had said, too. But what if my best wasn't enough?

Mum's voice came floating over the fence. 'Gary, are you over there? It's way past your bedtime.'

'Gotta go, Darcy. See ya later. Coming, Mum!'

'See ya, young'un,' said Darcy. 'Good luck for Satdy.'

The bedroom light was off. The other siblings were in bed, one of them was already snoring. I climbed up onto my bunk, and slipped under the covers.

'Good night, Bucky,' said Team-man.

Bucky. That was the best he could come up with. Bucky as in Bucky the Bucktooth Beaver.

It was so pathetic I didn't even bother replying. Just closed my eyes, and tried to sleep.

9

The only dentist I'd ever been to was at school, and she wasn't a proper dentist, only a DT, a dental therapist. She travelled around the peninsula with a caravan, visiting all the schools. She had thick glasses and her breath smelt like peppermint.

After giving me a couple of fillings she said, 'You know you should really see an orthodontist, get those front teeth straightened out. That's a severe occipital occlusion you've got there. Get it done now and you'll have a lovely smile for the rest of your life.'

'Yeth, ith shooth,' I said, which is what 'yes, I should' sounds like when your gums are numb.

She gave me a card with the address of an orthodontist on it. It was in town, of course. On that posh street where Team-man had to go after he busted his eardrum.

I knew I had a severe occipital occlusion. It wasn't as severe as Bucky Matic's, his teeth were just about at right-angles to his face, but I knew mine stuck out a bit. Every now and then somebody would stir me about it. The same old joke.

'Geez, mate, you could eat an apple through a bird cage.'

Funny, ha ha. The same old joke, but it still made you feel microscopic.

Whenever I looked in the mirror I remembered what the DT said, 'Get it done and you'll have a lovely smile for the rest of your life.'

Did I want a lovely smile for the rest of my life?

You betcha!

I wanted a smile just like Dumby Red's, a smile that made other people feel good. Dumby had never worn braces, he was just lucky I suppose, born with teeth that didn't stick out. Imagine having a smile like his, like a weapon. Things are going bad, you bring out the smile. Whammo! You're on top again.

I asked Mum. She was hanging out the washing.

'Mum, how much does it cost to go to the orthodentist?'

My poor Mum didn't have any teeth. She'd gone into hospital and they'd taken them all out, every last one. It was because of us kids. In her wedding photo, she's got this amazing smile, teeth all white and pearly, like she just stepped out of a Colgate ad. She always brushed them too, when she had them, and she never ate cake, or lollies, or ice-cream, or any of that crap. No, it was us kids. I read about it in a *Women's Weekly*. When a woman's pregnant the body takes calcium from the teeth to give to the baby in the womb. After eight kids I reckon there wasn't much calcium left in Mum's teeth, her body had taken it all. They became weak and rotten, so they took them out. They gave her falsies, of course, but she never got used to them. They spent more time in the top drawer of the kitchen cupboard than they did in her mouth. You'd be searching for something in the kitchen, open the drawer, and there they were, looking right at you. Scared the shit out of you, it did. But I never said anything to Mum. I felt a bit guilty.

'It's orthodontist, dear.'

'Okay, an orthodontist, but how much does it cost?'

'I don't know.'

'Is it expensive, or really expensive?'

'Why don't you ask your father when he comes home?'

I didn't. For a start I was always in bed when he came home. Besides, I knew what he'd say.

'Negative.'

Just like that mad robot in 'Lost in Space'.

'Negative, Will Robinson. Negative.'

10

'Coming up the oval for a few dobs?' asked Mark Arks as we got off the school bus.

He handballed a footy towards me. I went to grab it but my hands were still sore from the night before, from thumping the bloody thing, and it slipped through.

'Nuh, reckon I'll go home,' I said, watching the footy rolling down the road.

But instead I walked back down the main street, past Arks's shop and the old post office, until I came to the intersection where the main street met the coast road. I walked over to the anchor. It was a sort of memorial, I suppose, to the old days, when huge sailing ships called windjammers used to sail into the Port to load up with wheat and barley. Then they'd race back to

England. But as old Froggy used to say, and it was about all he ever said, 'Them days are gorn.' The anchor itself was huge, painted black and mounted on a concrete block. It was shiny on the top because little kids used to slide down it. Next to the anchor was a faded map. It was for the campers I suppose, so they didn't get lost. How anybody, even a camper, could get lost in the Port beats me. Either you were in the centre of the town or you weren't in the town at all. In front of the anchor, facing the sea, was a bench. I sat down.

It was an overcast day, and the sea was grey and lumpy looking, like old porridge. There was nobody on the jetty. It looked bored today, like it had nothing to do, just squat there on its thick wooden legs, and wait for a visitor.

I loved that jetty. I really did. I couldn't imagine the Port without it. I couldn't imagine living in the Port without it. If, for some reason, the jetty went, then so would I. I'd put all my belongings in one of those red hankies with the big white spots, tie it to a stick, and go out into the world in search of fame and fortune (and another jetty).

About three-quarters of the way up the jetty was the shed. That's what we called it anyway, though it was probably really a shelter, because one side of it was completely open. It was covered in graffiti, inside and out. Names of pop stars, football teams – all sorts of stuff. And we used to carve our initials into the wooden uprights with our pocket knives. It was sort of a tradition in our town. But only us boys did it. I'd never seen a girl carve her initials. Actually I'd never seen a girl write any graffiti. The only time a girl's name would appear was when one of us wrote it, like 'Monica is a slut' or 'Josie is slack'. One day somebody wrote 'Sharon B gives head'. It took me ages to scratch it out. I was so mad with Shaz, I didn't talk to her for ages.

To my right was the playground, the swings slowly twisting in the wind. In front of that the beach, piled high with seaweed. And out from there the boats, nodding at their moorings. My eyes followed the inward curve of the bay, past the caravan park, empty now in winter, past Black Rock, past the sandhills. I could just make out the Point in the distance.

I'd never been to the Point. And not because it was too far – it was only about three hours by foot. Once Dazza and I decided we were going to do it, walk along the coast, all the way there. We'd made it just past the sandhills and there was still plenty of time. But then we started thinking about those stories they told in the front bar – wild Nungas with spears, boomerangs that come from nowhere and knock you senseless. We got scared and ran all the way back to the Port.

From behind me came the sound of footsteps. I turned around. It was Pickles. He leaned against the anchor. He sniffed twice. He farted once. Then he started making that noise with his throat, which only Pickles could make, like he was dredging something up from his feet. The noise stopped. He rolled that something from cheek to cheek. Then he spat it out. I watched it fly through the air. It was green and horrible and it landed with a wet thud on the map.

After a while it started to move. Just missing the school, it ran slowly across the oval, slid along the highway for a while, then reached the edge, where it dropped off onto the gravel below.

Meet Pickles Mickle, one of my very bestest friends.

'You really the first ruck now?' he said.

'Seems like it,' I said.

'Christ!' he said.

'Thanks a lot, Pickles.'

Pickles was a hopeless footballer. There were plenty of Nungas not in the team who were better than him. But Pickles was from the Port, he was a local. And Shirl and Mick, his olds, bought their ciggies from Arks. Shirl and Mick smoked a lot of ciggies, they were probably Arks's best customers. So you couldn't drop Pickles for a Nunga. Pickles was always on the bench though. Sometimes, if we were well in front, Arks'd give him a run in the last quarter. But only if we were well in front, at least twenty goals.

Actually Pickles didn't really care, he wasn't that keen on playing anyway. But he liked to be in the team because you got to go to other towns on the weekend, and he could watch the girls play netball. He said it was because netball was an exciting and fast-moving game, but I knew he just wanted to perve on the girls' undies.

'I was thinking, we'll be dead-set heroes if we win, won't we?' he said.

'I s'pose.'

'Girls really go for heroes, don't they?'

Here we go, I thought. It's about to start.

'I don't know.'

'I'm telling you, they do. They'll be begging us for it.'

'Calm down, Pickles.'

'No, I'm telling you. They'll be all over us like a rash.'

'Mate, you've already got a rash.'

Pickles had the munga. Real bad. The munga, in case you don't know, is a fungus. It grows in warm damp places. Like Pickles' groin. He was always scratching at his munga. Pickles, we used to say, why dontcha buy some cream, get rid of that filthy munga? But he never did anything about it. He enjoyed the company, I reckon.

Pickles ignored my comment.

'If we win we'll be in like Flynn,' he said.

'Geez, Pickles, that's really poetic.'

'Nuh, I'm not kidding. We've gotta win this game.'

More responsibility. Now I was responsible for Pickles' pathetic sex life.

'By the way, did I tell ya, got me finger in down the bushes? That Kerley moll,' he said.

The bushes was a bit of sandy scrub, on the other side of the jetty, towards the boat ramp. People went there, late at night. Usually in pairs.

'She was beggin' for it, she was,' he added.

As usual he was lying. Pickles and his hyperactive sexual imagination. You should've heard him, the way he went on. Got a pash down the bushes. Got a bit of tit down the bushes. Got a finger down the bushes. Got pulled off down the bushes. Got this down the bushes. Got that down the bushes. The truth is that he got nothing down the bushes, no girl would go anywhere near the bushes with Pickles. Not even Mary Kerley and she'd been down the bushes with practically everybody (apparently).

Pickles wasn't exactly ugly. The problem was his personal hygiene. His hair was a rat's nest. He never cleaned his teeth – they always looked like he'd just eaten a bowl of pond slime. His fingernails were filthy. He farted constantly and a Pickles' fart would clear a room in five seconds flat. And his undies had more skid marks than the Grand Prix circuit.

So why did I hang around with him? I'm not sure. There weren't many kids my age in the Port. And his old man and my old man were fishing partners. And Pickles did have some good points, which I'll get to. Eventually.

Pickles and I sat there for a while, not saying anything. The clouds bunched up on the western horizon started to drift apart, and the sun appeared for the first time that day.

Pickles stood up, facing the sea, his hand shading his eyes.

'Here they come,' he said.

'Where?' I said.

'Over there,' he said, pointing.

I got up.

'So it is,' I said. 'I can see 'em too.'

I couldn't though. All I could see was water.

Pickles wasn't having me on either. Somewhere out there he could see the *Meryl*, the old man's boat. And I couldn't. It wasn't my eyesight. When they did those tests at school I could read the bottom line, the smallest letters, no problem. It was because Pickles was a fisherman. Sure, he went to school but that's only because the government made him. The day he turned fifteen he'd go fishing. Just like his father went fishing. And his grandfather went fishing. Pickles was born with saltwater in his blood.

There's no way I wanted to go fishing for the rest of my life. But somehow I was envious of Pickles. At least he knew what he'd do. Me, I didn't have the foggiest.

I could see the *Meryl* now, but only the wheelhouse, white against the dull brown of the island. If the boat headed straight for the moorings it meant they didn't have much of a catch, they'd be able to unload it into the dinghy, but if it was a big catch then they'd make for the jetty.

'They'll be pulling into the jetty,' said Pickles. 'They got amongst 'em.'

How the hell did he know that? I could only just see the boat and he was already telling me what sort of catch they had.

Sure enough the *Meryl* passed the jetty, then it swung around, slicing a wide arc in the water, and came alongside the ramp.

'Let's go see what they caught,' said Pickles.

'I've gotta go home.'

'Come on.'

'No really, I've gotta go. Mum's got some jobs for me.'

'You don't go nowhere near the boat no more, do ya?'

He was right. I didn't.

'I just gotta go,' I said.

'Ever since youse got caught in that southerly. It really put the shits up you, didn't it?'

'Something like that,' I said, and I turned around and walked away.

Did Pickles know what happened that night? I didn't think so. He knew about the storm, but that was all. He didn't know the rest. Only me and the old man did. Thank God.

But now I'm going to have to tell you what happened. I don't really want to. As Dumby would say, it shames me, brudda. But I've got no choice, it's part of the story, after all.

11

It happened a few months ago. It was a really warm day for early autumn. There was no wind, not a breath, and everything was hazy, like you were looking through an out-of-focus camera.

We'd slipped the moorings and were chugging past the jetty. A swell was running, but the sea was as smooth as glass.

The *Meryl*, the old man's boat, was a wooden thirty-footer. He'd found it, half sunk, on the other side of the peninsula, and done it up himself. I liked the *Meryl*, it reminded me of Darcy – it was old and slow, but it had a heap of character. The cabin was up front, and the wheelhouse was at the back, above the engine. The *Meryl* had a mast, even a sail, but the old man never used it. He didn't know the first thing about sailing.

Actually, he didn't know much about the ocean at all. He wasn't from the Port, he wasn't even from the country. He was a city boy, born and bred in the Big Smoke. That's why he went fishing with Mick. Mick had the know-how and the old man had the boat. It was a good partnership. But Mick had done his back, he couldn't come, so the old man had roped us in.

I was sitting on the bowsprit (that bit that sticks right out the front of the boat), my arm wrapped around the stay, my legs dangling over the side. Team-man was lying on the deck, watching the bow slice through the water. The boat lurched into a swell and my feet dipped into the sea.

'Watch out, there's a shark!' yelled Team-man.

I pulled my legs up even though I knew he was having me on, there was no shark.

'Sucked in,' he said, laughing.

It was Stephen Spielberg's fault. If I hadn't seen *Jaws* (three times), I would've kept my legs where they were.

I looked behind. The Port had become indistinct, a jumble of shapes and colours. Up ahead, to the right, the island sat low and flat.

'Dolphins!' said Team-man.

Three of them joined the boat. I watched their dark shapes zigzagging across the bow. Then they were gone.

'Where'd they go?' I said.

'Over there.'

The dolphins leaped into the air, their slick grey

flanks gleaming in the morning sun. They landed back in the water with a splash.

'Wow!' said Team-man.

'Wow!' I agreed.

It was going to be a great day, I could tell.

'Get that bait chopped up, can ya, Gary?' said the old man, stepping out of the wheelhouse, the gold cap on his front tooth glinting.

He's a big bloke, my old man. Well over six foot. Everybody said I had big bones. I was skinny but one day I'd fill out. But there was no way I'd ever be as big as the old man. Maybe as tall, but never as big, never as strong.

As usual he was wearing overalls, the sort that carpenters wear. The sleeves on his shirt were rolled up past his elbows. His thick, sandy hair was uncombed.

'And Tim, there's some lines that need untangling,' he added.

'Old man's in a good mood,' I said to Team-man.

'Why's that?'

'Called me Gary.'

'He's always in a good mood out here. It's only when you start tangling lines that he gets shitty.'

'Piss off.'

'It's true.'

Team-man liked to go fishing, he went every chance he could. Not me. I liked the boat, I liked the sea, I liked catching fish, but I didn't like it when the old man got angry, and when I went fishing he always seemed to get angry.

Mostly because of tangles. Lines and me just didn't get on. All I had to do was look at a line and it'd tangle. And it always happened at a critical moment, just when we'd hit a patch of fish. The others would be pulling them in, one after another, and I'd be sitting on the deck with a tangled line in my lap. Then the old man would start.

'Haven't you got that bloody thing untangled yet?'

And I'd get anxious. The more I tried to untangle the line, the worse it would get. The knots would get tighter and tighter.

Until finally he'd say, 'Give us the bloody thing here.'

He'd grab a knife, cut the tangle out, and knot the two ends back together.

'If I'm so hopeless,' I said to Team-man, 'why does he make me come out?'

'You know why,' said Team-man.

I did, too. I was lucky. Hopeless, but lucky. Whenever I went fishing, they caught heaps.

I got the bait out from the ice-box, a bag full of big eyes and squirmy tentacles. Squid, the best snapper bait you could get. Even Darcy wouldn't argue with that.

'Do you reckon what they say in the front bar is right, that wogs eat squid?' I asked Team-man as I decapitated a big one.

'Course it is. A wog'll eat anything. Even snails,' he said, tying a sinker onto the end of a line.

'I thought it was the froggies who ate snails, not the wogs.'

'Froggies, wogs, they're all the same, aren't they?'

'I s'pose.'

There were no wogs living in the Port, but sometimes wogs from town would come up the jetty. Continentals, Darcy called them, and didn't they get excited when we landed a squid. What did they call them again? Calamala? Carimari? Something like that. Maybe the front bar was right, they really did eat them.

By the time I'd finished chopping up all that squid, we were right out in the gulf. The land was out of sight.

The old man throttled back. I stood in the doorway of the wheelhouse watching the echo sounder as the needle traced a straight black line across the paper.

'Look at that, bottom's as flat as a tack,' said the old man.

He wasn't keen on flat as a tack. Neither were the snapper. They liked holes or ledges, and that's what the old man was looking for. Features, he called them. I looked at the compass. We were heading due west, out into the gulf, further away from the Port.

Suddenly the needle jagged upwards. A reef. A feature.

'Whoa!' said the old man, swinging the wheel hard. 'You boys get ready.'

I grabbed my line. The boat came back around.

'Now!' he said.

I dropped the sinker over the side of the boat. The line slipped through my hand, until it hit the bottom. Team-man did the same. Then we waited. And waited. And waited.

Until the old man said, 'Nothing, eh?'

'Not even a nibble,' said Team-man.

'Pull 'em in then, we'll try somewhere else.'

This went on all morning, the same pattern repeating over and over. The black line on the echo sounder would deviate from the horizontal, the old man would swing the boat around, we'd throw our lines over, and wait.

'This time, boys. This'll be the one.'

But it never was. If there were any snapper down there they weren't hungry, that's for sure. Or maybe they weren't keen on squid. I couldn't blame them for that. I wouldn't touch the stuff either.

It was mid-afternoon and we still hadn't caught a thing. The haze had lifted. It was clear now and hot, like a summer's day. The old man's good mood had gradually evaporated. He'd started drinking, tossing the empty stubbies over the side. I watched them bobbing in the wake. There was still no wind but a fat swell was rolling by. The boat kept heading west.

'We'll be on the other side of the gulf soon,' I said to Team-man.

'Is that land over there?' he said, pointing towards the horizon.

The sky there looked dirty and smudged, like the sink in the old man's shed.

I was no expert on the weather, but I'd sat on the jetty and listened to old Darcy plenty of times. The weather was one of his favourite topics, along with maggots and the war.

'That's not land. It's a change, and by the looks of it, it's headed this way. D'ya reckon the old man knows?'

'Of course he knows,' said Team-man.

But I wasn't so sure. Like I said before, the old man was a city boy, he didn't know the sea like Mick or Pickles or even Darcy did. And all day his eyes had been on that black line, and nothing else.

'You better tell him,' I said.

'No way. You go tell him,' said Team-man.

Just then the boat swung around again. The old man had found another one of his features.

'Lines in now,' he yelled from the wheelhouse door.

Best Team-man dropped his line over. I watched it slip through his hand, droplets of water flying off as the sinker sped towards the bottom. Then it stopped.

'Got one!' he yelled, almost immediately.

I threw my line in. As it hit the bottom, a fish took the bait. The line bit into my hands.

'Me too!'

Team-man gave his line a mighty heave, and a huge snapper landed flapping on the deck.

The fish on my line was big, too. It was taking all my strength to pull it in. Finally I landed it. Another snapper, bigger than Team-man's, the biggest fish I'd ever caught.

'Get the hook out of it,' said the old man. 'Before it tangles the line.'

He'd dropped the anchor, and was just about to throw his line over.

I knelt down, leaning on the snapper's head with my forearm, and guided the hook out of its mouth. Then I pushed it into the well.

'Got one,' said the old man. 'You little beauty!'

'So have I,' said Team-man.

I rebaited the hook and threw my line in. Down deep I could see a silvery-pink flash. I felt a tug.

'Me, too,' I said.

Then the line started ripping out of my hands.

'It's too big. I can't hold it!'

'Give it here,' said the old man.

He wrapped my line around his left hand. The nylon cut deep into the skin. He didn't flinch.

'Take this one,' he said, handing me his line.

I'd hit patches before, but not like this one. These snapper were monsters, and they were ravenous. They were flying up from the bottom, not even waiting for the bait to reach them. Almost as soon as I threw my line in one of them would take it. I'd pull it in, or if it was too big, the old man would. I'd take the hook out and push the fish into the well. Then I'd rebait, and throw the line over again. Another monster would take it. They didn't stop.

My back was sore, my arms were aching and my hands were cut to shreds.

'Anybody wanna drink?' I said.

'Yeah, me,' said Team-man.

The old man said nothing.

As I got the water from the ice-box, I looked up at the sky. It was as black as squid ink.

'Have you seen the sky?' I asked the old man.

His shirt was soaked with sweat. He hadn't stopped all afternoon, hadn't slowed down. Fish after fish after fish he'd pulled in. Like a machine.

'What?' he said, annoyed.

'The sky. I reckon there might be a storm coming.'

He looked up. I knew he hadn't noticed it before.

'Nothing in it,' he said. 'Bit of a blow, that's all.'

'But haven't we got enough fish, anyway?' I said. 'The well's full.'

'Enough!' he repeated, incredulously.

Another snapper smacked onto the deck.

'We're not fishing for a feed, you know. These are dollar bills we're pulling in. Enough, my arse. Keep on fishing!'

I dropped my line into the water.

'Please, Mr Snapper,' I said under my breath. 'Go away. I'll tell you a little secret – there's a nasty sharp hook hidden inside that scrummy-looking piece of squid. And what about your friends? Haven't you noticed that they're all disappearing? Please, Mr Snapper, go away.'

Another moronic fish grabbed the bait. Slowly, I started reefing it in. Suddenly there was less weight on the line.

That's strange, I thought. They don't usually get off, not these kamikaze fish.

I pulled the line in. There was a head on the end.

That's all – just the fish's head, the body had been bitten off.

Then Team-man pulled in a head. So did the old man.

'Noahs. That's the end of that,' said the old man. 'Looks like we're going anyway.'

Stephen Spielberg really did have a lot to answer for. He'd given sharks a bad name, and they didn't deserve it. Not these sharks anyway. They'd rescued me from a pack of monster snapper.

Team-man winched the anchor up. The old man started the engine. A plume of black smoke shot out from the exhaust and the smell of diesel filled the air.

'Get me a coupla stubbies, can ya?' said the old man.

I got them from the ice-box.

'I tell you what, there's nothing to this fish caper,' he said, and took a huge swig of beer, almost emptying the bottle.

'Money for old rope it is. Money for old rope.'

'What about the storm?' I said. The sky was blacker now, more threatening. A breeze had sprung up, ruffling the water. And we were at least five hours from the Port.

'Christ, you're a worrier, ain't ya? I told you it's nothing, bit of a blow, that's all.'

He took another swig and flicked the stubby over the side.

He was probably right. A bit of a blow, that's all. Nothing to get worried about. What I needed was some shut-eye. The air inside the cabin was old and stale and I was covered in stinking fish slime, but I was too exhausted to care. I lay on the bunk, fully clothed, and closed my eyes. The boat was rocking now. Gently, like a cradle. I soon fell asleep.

I dreamt of snapper. A giant one had pulled me off the boat, and down through the water, to the bottom, to the ledge. There was a mob of them down there, and they weren't happy.

'Where are our friends? Where are our friends?' they were yelling, showing their huge teeth. And they were closing in on me . . .

Then I woke up. I was on the floor. I'd been thrown out of my bunk. The boat was pitching and rolling. The cabin was leaking, water dripping from the windows where the sealant had been shaken loose. My clothes were wet. There was a terrible smell. I got up.

Best Team-man was on the other bunk, moaning. His face was white. There was a pool of vomit on the floor next to him.

'You okay?' I asked.

'Where are we?' he said.

I put my face against the porthole. It was dark outside, all I could see was water foaming against the glass.

'Who knows?' I said, then the boat pitched suddenly and I was thrown back onto the floor.

Then Team-man tumbled out of his bunk. He landed on top of me.

'Sorry,' he said, and he dragged himself back up.

'That's okay,' I said.

I looked at the clock, six hours since we pulled the anchor up. Christ! We should be home by now.

I opened the cabin hatch. The wind, full of spray, blasted into my face. The boat slid down a trough and an enormous wave smashed onto the deck. I'd been in storms before, but nothing like this – the boat was being tossed around like it was one of the old man's stubbies. I looked around. No lights. Nothing but waves. Huge waves with foaming crests. It was terrifying.

I could see the old man, framed by the window, standing in the wheelhouse. Through the spray, in the dim glow of the deck lights, he looked half-human. There was a grotesque smile on his face. Like he was enjoying it, enjoying the challenge.

I grabbed the safety rail and pulled myself along the deck. Another wave smashed on the deck. The water churned around my thighs. When I got to the wheelhouse I pushed the door open.

'Where are we?' I screamed. It was almost impossible to talk above the clatter of the engine.

The old man said nothing, his eyes were glued to the compass. He wrestled with the wheel as the boat lurched into another mountainous wave.

'Where are we?' I screamed, as loud as I could.

Still he said nothing, but pointed towards the cabin.

Then we got hit side-on. The boat rolled viciously. I was flung into the wheelhouse, against the old man, knocking his hands from the wheel. The boat kept going over and over, until it was almost on its side.

'It's not gunna stop, it's not gunna stop,' I was yelling. But at last, when the mast was almost parallel to the surface, it rolled the other way. Both of us were thrown against the other side of the wheelhouse. The old man grabbed the wheel.

'You're trying to kill us!' I screamed.

Warm tears were sliding down my wet face.

'Get back in that cabin,' yelled the old man.

'You're trying to kill us! You hate us!'

With one hand the old man grabbed me by the front of the shirt.

'Get back in that fucking cabin,' he said, and he shoved me through the doorway.

The boat rolled and I went flying into the safety rail, my momentum almost catapulting me over. Then it went the other way and I was thrown sprawling onto the deck. I crawled, on hands and knees, the water streaming around me, back to the hatch and dropped into the cabin.

I got back on the soaking bunk. Team-man was on the floor. He was dry-retching now, his body heaving. The smell in the cabin was putrid.

'Where are we?' he said weakly.

'We're gunna die,' I said.

I believed it, too. The next time the boat rolled would be the last time. We'd keep on going, all the way to the bottom, to Davey Jones's locker.

I soon got tossed out of the bunk again. This time I stayed there, wedged in next to Team-man. I could feel his vomit, warm and sticky, against my cheek. I didn't care.

Somehow, I don't know how, I went to sleep. When I woke the boat was steady. I opened the hatch. The water was much calmer. I could see a lighthouse flashing in the distance. We were behind the island, almost home.

The old man said nothing as we moored the boat. Nothing as we rowed into the beach. Nothing as we got into the car. Team-man collapsed onto the back seat.

I sat in the front. The sun was just coming up.

'I never want you on my boat again,' he said, slowly, emphatically.

I didn't say anything.

'Do you hear me? I never want you on my boat again.'

'Okay,' I said, softly.

Then he shook his head and started the car.

'My own son a gutless wonder. A gutless fucking wonder.'

I rubbed my forehead. I'd never felt so ashamed in all my life.

And I hadn't been on the boat since that day. I hadn't been anywhere near the boat since that day.

12

After I left Pickles, I walked along the coast. First along the beach, the rich tang of rotting kelp in my nostrils, then onto the rocks. Most of the coast around the Port was rocky, which was fine by me. Beaches are okay, but let's face it, they're dead. Nothing lives in sand, except maybe a few worms. But rocks, they're teeming with life. Look in any rock pool, you'll see urchins, starfish, anemones, crabs, fish, sponges – all sorts of animals, a whole community.

I stopped when I got to Black Rock. Us Blacks owned Black Rock. Not legally of course, but it was straight down from our place and we used to hang out there all the time. Especially at high tide it looked like a giant naked Nunga about to duck dive. Two great big black cheeks and a weedy crack sticking out of the water. I wanted people to call Black Rock 'Bum Rock' (or at least 'Black Bum Rock') because in my opinion its bumness was greater than its blackness.

'Coming down Bum Rock for a swim?' I'd ask a sibling.

'Where?' they'd reply.

'Bum Rock, you know – used to be Black Rock,' I'd explain.

'Oh, Black Rock, why didn't you say? Sure I'll come.'

It was hopeless.

I scrambled up the sandy cliff and onto the road. The siblings were having kicks, end to end. Jenny had the footy.

'There he is, the first ruck,' she said when she saw me.

She kicked the ball. An immaculate drop punt hit me square on the chest.

'Over here,' said Kevin. 'Kick it to me.'

I took careful aim. The ball flew high over Kevin's head and bounced off Darcy's mailbox.

I tell you, it was getting more and more difficult to believe in God. Mrs Ashburner, my old Sunday School teacher, said that God was kind and just. Maybe, but why did he make my sister a better kick than me? It didn't add up.

I went inside.

Mum was in the laundry, leaning on the washing machine, a book propped up in front of her. The machine was shaking and the book was jumping about. Didn't worry Mum, though. She was used to it. She spent a lot of time in the laundry. I suppose it was inevitable with a family as big as ours. But I also think the laundry was a kind of sanctuary for Mum, where she could get away from us lot for a while. None of us liked to go there, not with that smell. It used to be worse, when the three little ones were in nappies, but Team-man still wore socks.

I couldn't see the title of the book but I knew it was a Mills and Boon romance, an M&B. That's all my mum read, apart from magazines like *Women's Weekly* and *Woman's Day*.

'Hi, Mum,' I said.

'Hello, dear,' she said.

I could see the title now – *A Circle of Opals*.

'That's a good book, isn't it?' I said.

I'd started reading it in the toilet that morning. Mum left her M&Bs all over the place, in the kitchen, in the laundry, in the bathroom, in the toilet – especially in the toilet. And if you're sitting on the dunny, not doing much, and there's an M&B just sitting there, then of course you're going to read it. It's screaming out to you, 'read me, read me, pick me up and read me'. How can you resist?

'Haven't you got schoolbooks to read?' she said

Mum wanted me to read books that improved my mind.

'I've read them,' I said.

Which was true.

She turned the page.

'Mum,' I said.

'Yes.'

'Do you reckon Opal will find true happiness with the dark stranger Zac Heynes? And what is that glamorous Mari up to?'

She gave me a dirty look (even dirtier than the clothes on the floor), closed the book, and slipped it into her apron.

Mum was a really fast reader, she just gobbled up the pages. She was about halfway through *A Circle of Opals*; tomorrow she'd finish and take it back to the library. I'd never get to finish it. This happened all the time, I'd start a M&B but I wouldn't get to finish it. This worried me a bit, because I'd read this article at the barber's, in a *People* magazine, about this kid who committed all these robberies. When he got caught he said he didn't realise that he'd get into trouble, because his parents made him go to bed at eight on the dot, so he only got to watch half of whatever cop show was on the telly. He never saw the end, with the car chase, where the villain got caught and sent to jail. It got me thinking. Maybe I'd have a similar problem when I got older and started having love affairs. I'd be really good at the first bit, the 'she met his steely gaze' stuff, but I'd be hopeless later on, because I hadn't read those chapters.

The machine clicked into spin mode.

'Are you all ready for Saturday?' asked Mum.

'I think so. Who's coming?' I said.

'Practically the whole town,' she said.

'The old ... I mean, Dad's coming, isn't he?'

The old man wasn't too interested in the footy. The only advice he ever gave was 'make sure you come off the ground exhausted', which didn't really make a lot of sense. Normally I didn't care if he came or not, but I really wanted him to go to the grand final. I don't know why, maybe I wanted to show him that I wasn't so gutless after all.

'He said he was, dear.'

'But last night he didn't even remember it was on when Tim asked him.'

'Your father's got a lot on his plate.'

'Got a lot in his glass more like it,' I said.

The machine stopped spinning.

Uh oh, I thought, she's gunna crack a wobbly. Mum didn't often crack a wobbly, but when she did, it was a very wobbly wobbly.

'That's enough of that sort of talk,' she said. 'Come on. Give me a hand to hang these out.'

'Sure, Mum.'

She opened the machine, and pulled out a tangle of clothes. I grabbed the basket.

One day, I promised myself, I'm going to ask her – what did you marry him for? Why did you make all those kids? Of course there's nothing wrong with all those kids. One of them is me, after all. And some of the siblings are quite presentable, but still, you've gotta wonder. They just didn't seem to have much in common, my olds. Not from the start.

I'd seen this photo of the old man. I s'pose he was about twenty, something like that. He's sitting on a motorbike, and he's wearing a leather jacket. And even though the motorbike is really old-fashioned looking and the leather jacket is pretty daggy, there's something about him. He looks tough. If you were a bloke and you saw him roaring down the street you'd think – No way I'd pick him. But if you were a girl I reckon you'd think something else.

Actually this photo of the old man reminded me of this kid at school called Jimmy Downes.

I reckon there're three types of tough. There're kids like Pickles who act tough, but they're not. There're kids who don't act tough, but they are. Like the Thumper. And there're a few kids, not very many, who act tough and are tough. Jimmy Downes was one of these.

He was always in trouble. Always getting the cuts. He'd even been expelled for a while. Then he started going with Sarah Goodkin. Sarah Goodkin's old man was filthy rich, a doctor or bank manager or something. She was a senior prefect, she was top of her class, and she was really good at sport. You'd think she'd be the last person to go for Jimmy Downes. But she did. Did she ever. This one time I was in the dunnies and I heard Jimmy Downes telling some other kids about what he did to Sarah Goodkin after the school social. Except he didn't say 'did to Sarah Goodkin', he said 'done to Sarah Goodkin', just like my old man would say it.

13

The night before the grand final. I couldn't sleep. I was nervous, excited. Tossing and turning, my bed felt too small. The sheets and the blankets were all messed up.

I tried counting sheep. One sheep. Two sheep. The third sheep was enormous, it had the Thumper's face. I stopped counting sheep.

I needed something. Something to help me sleep. Maybe Mum would give me one of her pills. The little ones she kept on the side of her bed.

I got out of bed and tip-toed along the corridor. The bathroom door was closed, but I could see light seeping under the door. Then I heard a soft splash. Mum was having a bath, getting some of her beloved peace and quiet. I looked out the window, the old man's car wasn't there. It was late, probably past midnight, but Mum would stay up until he came home, so she could serve him his dinner. She always did this.

'Mum,' I said.

'Who's that?'

'It's me, Mum, Gary. I can't sleep. Can I have one of your little pills?'

'No you can't. Wait a minute and I'll make you a nice cup of Milo.'

More splashes.

'It's all right. You stay there, Mum. I can do it.'

The house felt really strange this time of the night. Eerie. I wasn't used to it being so quiet. Everybody asleep except Mum and me. Seven kids sleeping, not making a noise, is a lot quieter than one or two.

I put the pot on the stove, filled it with milk, and turned on the element. Then I put a teaspoon of Milo and two teaspoons of sugar into a cup. The milk didn't take long to boil. I filled the cup and gave it a good stir. I took it into the lounge room and switched on the light. All the Best Team-man trophies, the little silver men, stopped what they were doing and stared at me. What's he doing in here this time of night?

There were hardly any books in our house. Mum always took her M&Bs back to the library, to swap for more, and the old man only ever read the form guide. But we did have *Great Finals in Football History*. I'd read it so often I knew some parts off by heart.

I opened it at my favourite chapter. The 1970 grand final. Carlton versus Collingwood. At half-time Carlton were down by 44 points. Then the great Ron Barassi told his players to go handball happy. They did, and the rest is football history. Carlton won and modern football was changed forever. There's a big photo of Jezza taking the mark of the century. I gazed at it, sipping my Milo. How could somebody get so high? Jezza was practically standing on the other bloke's head. It didn't seem possible. Like it was against the laws of physics. I don't know whether it was the Milo or Jezza's mark, but I felt calmer now.

Mum was still in the bath. I knocked on the door.

'Yes.'

'Mum, I'm feeling better now,' I said.

'Good,' she said. 'You get some sleep. You'll need it.'

I climbed back up onto my bunk. Below me Kevin was snoring. I could feel the Milo, warm inside me. I soon fell asleep.

14

I woke up. At first it seemed like any other day; light streaming in through the window, a kookaburra outside cackling madly, and the whiff of Team-man's socks drifting up from the floor. Then I remembered. Football. Grand final. Wangaroo. The Thumper. Today. Shit-a-brick!

As I sat up I could feel them in my tummy. Butterflies. They were flying around in there, a squadron of them. Loop the looping, spiral diving, formation flying. It was a veritable air-show.

Why am I doing this? I thought to myself. Why am I putting myself through this torture? Nobody has to play football. It's entirely voluntary. So why am I doing it? For the glory of it. That's what Arks would say. The glory. It was a strange word, especially for Arks. It didn't go with the rest of his vocabulary. It made me think of the war, the Anzacs. Our glorious men going over the top at Gallipoli. Did they feel like this? Did they have squadrons of butterflies vrooming around their tummies? The Anzacs were going to meet the dreaded Turk and probably death. I was going to meet the dreaded Thumper and probably death.

I had a long shower, the taps on full, the water blasting against my skin. Nobody bashed on the door, which was unusual. In our family if you got two minutes undisturbed in the shower you were lucky. But I suppose the siblings had been up and running about for ages already.

Then I got dressed. The clothes I usually wore to the footy — jeans, t-shirt and a black windcheater.

'Morning,' I said as I sat down at the kitchen table.

There was enough food to feed the whole team. Snags. Eggs. Bacon. Tomato. A mountain of toast, already buttered. Even apricot jam. What a luxury. It was usually dark plum from the tin. But this was apricot from the jar.

'Morning, dear,' said Mum.

Best Team-man was already tucking in, tomato sauce slurped all over the place. His plate looked like a road accident.

'Where's everybody?' I said.

'Around the place,' said Mum. 'Getting ready.'

'What about Dad?'

'He's still sleeping. He had a late night.'

Mum put a plate in front of me.

'There you go,' she said.

I looked down. Mum had attempted to recreate Mt Kosciusko using nothing but common foodstuffs. There were three snags, two tomatoes, two fried eggs and about a pig's worth of bacon.

'Thanks, Mum,' I said, trying to sound sincere.

Actually, a couple of Weetbix would've done me fine, but Mum had gone to all that trouble, so I had to eat some of it.

I took a mouthful of bacon. It plummeted into the airfield, causing two butterflies to collide. I tried a bit of snag. Another mid-air collision resulted. I resisted further bombardment. Instead I sipped some milky tea.

'You haven't touched your food,' said Mum.

'I'll have it,' said Team-man.

He leant across the table, and swiped my plate.

'I'm not feeling too flash,' I said. 'I might go and lie down for a while.'

'Not too long. We'll get going soon,' said Mum.

'But Mum, the game doesn't start until two!'

'You know I like to be early.'

I sure did. It didn't matter what the occasion was – wedding, funeral, final – Mum'd be the first one there. Being early was a religion to her.

I lay down on the sofa. Were the siblings hyped up, or what? They were running around all over the place, in and out of doors. It looked like a Marx Brothers' movie. They'd blown up balloons, tied streamers onto sticks, and made a banner from an old sheet. 'PORT FOR PREMEIRS' it said.

'That's not how you spell "premiers",' I said.

'Isn't it?' said Kevin. 'Too late now. We're gunna tie it to the fence. Right next to you.'

'Thanks a lot, Kev.'

Then Mum said, 'Okay, let's go!'

By the time me and my squadron of butterflies got outside, the car was packed.

You know that old joke – how d'ya get four elephants into a Mini Minor?

If you don't then get ready to piss yourself because the answer's pretty hilarious.

Two in the front seat, two in the back seat.

Okay, well here's another one.

How d'ya get ten Blackies into a car?

You probably said five in the front and five in the back, but I haven't told you that the Blackymobile is a station-wagon.

So the correct answer is four in the front (two adults, siblings seven and eight), four in the back seat (siblings one to four) and two right in the back (siblings five and six).

Except today there were only nine of us.

'Is Dad ready?' I said as I squeezed in.

'He'll be a while yet,' said Mum.

'But isn't he coming with us?'

'No, he'll come later.'

'But how will he get there?'

'The whole of the Port's going, there'll be no shortage of rides.'

'Are you sure he's coming?'

'I'm sure,' she said, adjusting the seat so it was all the way forward. Then she started the engine.

The siblings cheered. We were off.

The finals were in Wangaroo. The finals were always in Wangaroo. Because of their facilities, which were second to none. I'd like a Pollywaffle for every time somebody from Wangaroo had said to me, 'Our facilities – second to none, mate.' I think they must've learnt it at a very early age.

I have to admit – their oval was green and lush. Ours was brown and dusty. It never got watered, the club couldn't afford it, the funds weren't there. Our change rooms were a bit rough, too. Dirt floors, cold showers. Nails for hangers. Visiting teams were always whinging about it. Wangaroo had tiled floors and hot showers. I suppose they were right – second to none.

So Wangaroo had the home-ground advantage. Another fact of life – never underestimate the importance of the home-ground advantage.

We arrived early, of course. There was nobody at the gate so we got in for nothing. But being early wasn't about saving money. Later Mum would send a sibling over with the entrance fee. Being early was about being early.

Mum parked the car in her favourite place, just around from the goals, between the forward-pocket and the half-forward flank. The siblings piled out. There were only a few people around. A man was trundling a funny-looking machine around the edge of the oval, marking the boundary line with white paint. Three blokes were erecting a beer tent – they always put an extra one up for the finals. A white van pulled up next to the canteen. 'Wangaroo Bakery' it said on the side.

What a day for footy! It was perfect – cool, and the sky was clear with just a few wispy clouds up high. There was no wind either.

Mum unscrewed the thermos and poured a cup of tea. Then she took a pen and started on 'Mr Wisdom's Whopper', her favourite crossword.

'Come on, let's have a dob,' said Best Team-man.

He ran onto the oval, bouncing the ball, dodging imaginary tackles. Then he kicked the ball, aiming for a couple of magpies pecking around in the grass.

'Leave 'em alone,' I shouted.

The birds flew off as the ball bounced next to them. They landed on the branch of a gum tree behind the goals.

'At least they're wearing black and white, our colours,' I said.

'Yeah, but I betcha they still barrack for Wangaroo,' said Best Team-man.

'Jezza on the lead,' I yelled, running into space.

Team-man kicked the ball out in front of me. I marked it on my chest. Then I looked up, took two steps and kicked. The ball took off like a rocket and soared over the goals.

'That's it,' I said walking back to the car.

'What do you mean, that's it?' said Best Team-man 'We just got out here. That was a great dob.'

'I know it was, that's why I have to stop. If I use up

all my great dobs now, I won't have any left for the match.'

'Don't be stupid.'

'I'm not being stupid. It's mathematics. Probability.'

'Kicking a football is probability?'

'Sure. It's like this. I'm not the greatest kick, right? I'll be the first to admit that. Maybe one out of ten kicks will be any good. So probability is that the next nine will be shithouse.'

'Then just have nine quick kicks and start all over again.'

'Geez, you're hopeless at maths. Probability doesn't work like that. Maybe the next nine kicks will be good. Then I will have stored up ninety bad kicks, and I won't have time before the match to use them up.'

'Then mean to kick badly.'

'No, you can't do that, you can't trick probability. Don't you know that's why casinos make stacks of money, because you can't trick probability?'

'Then why did you even bother coming out for a dob?'

'In case I did ninety bad kicks, then I'd have ten good ones all ready for the game.'

'Fair dinkum,' said Team-man, shaking his head in disgust. He hated that, when I beat him with pure and impeccable logic.

As I walked back to the car, a dusty white ute pulled up alongside Mum. Bales of hay in the back, a pointy-nosed sheep-dog running from one side to the other, barking. Grills Lillee was driving. He always parked next to Mum. Sitting in the passenger seat was Grills Lillee's son, also called Grills Lillee. All the male Lillees (and some of the female Lillees) were called Grills. Don't ask me why, I don't think even the Lillees knew. Some sort of family tradition I suppose. It got a bit confusing, so we called the son 'Young'un Grills'. But 'Young'un Grills' had three brothers and each of them was called 'Young'un Grills'. Luckily they weren't with the other Grills Lillees today. They were probably back on the farm, feeding the chooks, or watering the sheep, or whatever it is that farmers do.

Grills leant across and wound the window down. He looked like all farmers – big horsy teeth, face red from the sun, and a haircut he'd given himself with his wool clippers.

'Gidday, Mrs Black,' he said.

Grills talked like all farmers, too. By using the squeeze technique. It was because of all those flies out in the bush. Open your mouth, and you'd end up with one down your throat. Not a pleasant experience, I can assure you. So farmers like Grills didn't open their mouths, they squeezed out words from a little chink in the side. But they got so used to it, they did it all the time, even when the chance of getting a fly in the throat was minimal. Squeezing out words was a very slow process. In the time it took Grills Lillee to say, 'Gidday, Mrs Black,' most people would've carried out a fairly decent conversation.

'Gidday, Mr Lillee,' replied Mum.

'Nice day for it,' squeezed Grills.

93

'Perfect,' said Mum.

That was it. Grills didn't say anything after that. He probably wouldn't for the rest of the day. It was hard work squeezing out words. That's why Grills sat in his ute all day. That's why he didn't go over to the beer tent with the rest of the blokes and abuse the mug-rotten umpires. That's why he beeped his horn so much.

The siblings had run off in all directions. Two of them were tying the banner to the fence. I lay down on the back seat.

'Are you feeling okay, dear?' said Mum.

'I'm all right, just a bit nervous,' I said.

I closed my eyes. The sun was level with the window now, its warmth filtering through onto my face. It was quiet, only the sound of Mum's pen scratching away on 'Mr Wisdom's Whopper'. I was drifting off.

Ka – bang!!

An exhaust backfired. A car pulled up next to ours. I sat up. It was a station-wagon, full of rust, a bunch of black and white streamers tied to the aerial. In the front sat Shirl and Mick, and in the back was Pickles.

'It's Shirl and Mick!' I said.

'It's not,' said Mum, looking up from the crossword. 'Blast,' she said under her breath.

You probably don't rate 'blast' very high as far as swear words go. Maybe you don't even think it is a swear word. But my mum did. According to her, 'blast' was right up there. It was strong language indeed. She wasn't happy.

'Gidday,' said Mick, getting out of the car.

Mick was a skinny little bloke, but hard work had made him tough and sinewy. Years ago he'd got cancer of the left ear, so the doctors had chopped it off. They'd given him a false one, but Mick didn't like it; he never wore it. Instead he'd pull his beanie (always a black and white one) down on one side, to cover the hole. We'd all gotten used to it, but it must've looked pretty weird to anybody else. Mick had dressed up for the occasion – he was wearing tight brown trousers, a wide belt with a serious buckle, a white nylon shirt and his best thongs. Even his beanie looked clean.

He was rolling a cigarette. Once Mick put a rollie in his mouth, it didn't come out, that's where it stayed, stuck to his bottom lip, even when he talked. Mick didn't talk that much anyway, and when he did it was usually only a single word like 'yep' or 'nup' or 'dunno'.

Shirl got out from the other side.

'Gidday, Gwen,' she said to Mum.

'Gidday, luv,' to me.

Shirl reminded me of the cuttlefish shells we collected from the beaches. She was sort of frail and sunbleached. Her eyes were blue, but a faint blue, the colour of your favourite t-shirt that's been washed over and over. She was wearing an old footy jumper. It came down to her knees. Below that her skinny legs stuck out.

'Have a feed of prawns with us and a beer won't ya, Gwen?' said Shirl, lighting up a ciggie.

'Yes, I'd love that,' said Mum.

She was lying.

Shirl and Mick hardly ever came to the footy but when they did, they didn't muck about, they made a big day of it. Mick set up two deck chairs in front of the car, just behind the boundary line. He struggled by with an enormous esky. He put it between the two chairs. Then they both sat down. Mick fished two stubbies out of the esky. He handed one to Shirl. In perfect unison, like synchronised swimmers, they tore the tops off, raised the stubbies to their mouths, and took a sip.

'Imagine,' said Mum softly, looking up from her crossword. 'At this time of the day.'

'We passed Arks,' said Pickles. 'He'll be here soon.'

As if on cue the Arksmobile farted into the ground. I could see the Nungas jumping up and down in the back. I could hear them laughing and yelling.

It pulled in next to the Grills. I couldn't see Dumby anywhere.

Immediately I thought the worst – Dumby's not coming. Something happened to him. First we lose Colin (who used to be Carol). Now Dumby. May as well just hand the trophy over to Thumper. Don't even bother playing.

'Where's Dumby?' I asked Clemboy.

'Coming with his mob. Be here dreckly,' he said.

Thank God for that. But who was Dumby's mob? I didn't even know Dumby had a mob. He always got a lift to the footy with Arks.

'Here they come now.'

A late-model Holden Torana, covered in thick red

dust, came through the gates. It stopped on the other side of the oval.

'Why don't they park here?

'Search me,' said Clemboy. 'Why don't you go arks 'em?'

By the way – the Arks family weren't the only ones who said arks.

'Come on, let's go see them,' I said to Pickles.

'Nah, you go. He's your mate, not mine.'

I walked around the boundary. Past all the cars with Wangaroo colours. There were plenty of filthy looks and a few muttered comments. One little kid even tried to trip me up. I was behind enemy lines here, that's for sure. It was a relief to get to Dumby's car. He was standing at the back, looking good as usual, wearing his favourite boots with the red stars. There was a girl next to him. Somehow she looked familiar. Then two men got out of the front.

'Hey, Dumby. I didn't think you were coming. I was getting worried,' I said.

He smiled.

'Don't worry about me, brudda. Mr Reliable. Hey, this here is my little sis, Clarence. This is Blacky.'

'Gidday,' she said.

Then I realised where I'd seen her – playing netball. I used to go and watch my sisters play. (Not to perve on the girls' undies like Pickles, honest.) I remembered Clarence because she was so good. She was short, but quick. Sometimes too quick for her team-mates – they wouldn't be ready for her passes, the ball would fly past them. Clarence. That's right, the other players called her 'Clar'. Good pass, Clar. Well done, Clar. But I didn't know she was Dumby's sister.

'Gidday,' I said.

'And this is me dad,' said Dumby.

'Pleased to meet ya,' he said, holding out his hand. 'Chug-a-lug.'

Dumby and his old man were like peas in a pod. Except one of the peas had grown a fair-sized beer gut. He looked pretty fit though, like he could still pull on the boots and play a decent game of footy (as long as he didn't have to run around too much). He was a flashy dresser, too. He was wearing white shoes and a cowboy hat. There were a couple of huge rings on his fingers and a chunky gold watch on his wrist.

'Good day for the footy, Mr Red,' I said, shaking his hand.

Dumby and Clarence laughed.

'I ain't no mister,' he said, smiling. The same killer smile as Dumby. 'Call me Tommy. Chug-a-lug.'

'And that's my Uncle Sid,' said Dumby.

Uncle Sid was looking out at the oval. He looked around, over his shoulder, when Dumby said his name.

'Gidday,' he said, and he turned his gaze back to the oval.

Then Arks's voice came floating across the oval. 'All youse Port players. Get over here. Now!'

'I think he wants us,' said Dumby.

'I think he might,' I said.

Dumby grabbed his bag from the back of the car.

'Good luck, youse two,' said Clarence. 'I'll be cheering for youse.'

My face went red. Well, I think it went red. It felt like it went red.

'Chug-a-lug,' said Tommy.

By now all our players had arrived. They were standing around the Arksmobile. There were plenty of dads there, too. I looked around but I couldn't see mine, not even over at the beer tent.

'I want us all to sit together in the stand,' said Arks. 'No wandering off. Watch the first half of the Under 12s' game. I want youse to watch which way the ball bounces, see what the wind's doing. Let's go now.'

Dumby and I sat together. He started combing his hair.

Then the Thumper walked past. He was wearing shorts and a truckie's singlet. He had a pie in each hand. He took a bite from one, then the other.

'Geez, he's got bigger,' said Deano.

'Look at the size of those arms,' said Clemboy.

'Imagine the tatts he could fit on them,' said Pickles. It was Pickles's dream to get a tatt.

'Be quiet you guys, he might hear you,' I said.

'Hey, Thumper,' yelled Dumby.

'Shut up, Dumby,' I said.

The Thumper kept on walking. Thank God he didn't know he was the Thumper.

'Wangaroo first ruck. Up here,' yelled Dumby, louder this time.

The Thumper stopped, and looked up towards us in

99

the stand. He didn't say anything, but he had that stance – legs apart, elbows slightly out, like those gun-slingers in the old westerns. Instead of six-shooters he had meat pies, but he was still dangerous. I elbowed Dumby in the ribs.

'Best team win, unna,' said Dumby, smiling.

Thumper smiled back. Bits of pie crust between his teeth.

Then, in a voice as deep as the graves he dug, he said, 'Yeah, best team win,' and kept on walking.

'What you do that for?' I said to Dumby.

'Why not?' he answered.

It was typical of Dumby. He was always doing things like this. Mad things that had no meaning.

The siren went. Half-time. Murraculka Under 12s were leading Tangaratta Under 12s by eleven points. Big deal.

'Okay, lads, let's go,' said Arks. 'Time to get ready.'

'PORT' said the handwritten sign on the change room's door. Wangaroo's facilities may have been second to none, but the smell was the same, like all change rooms – sweat, dirty socks, liniment oil.

By the time I'd finished changing, that squadron of butterflies had resumed their aerial manoeuvres. I wasn't the only one who was nervous, though. I looked at my team-mates spread around the room. Some were sitting down, heads between their knees, others were pacing back and forth, like lions in a cage, others were bounc-ing footies against the wall. Even Dumby had tied and untied his bootlaces about ten times already.

But Arks was more nervous than all of us. He had a piece of chalk in his hand and was attacking the black-board like a mad man. 'Chalking out the tactics' he called it. When he'd finished it looked like a kid's scribble from kindy. I don't know why he bothered. Let's face it, Arks only had one tactic – 'down the guts'. I suppose he had 'kick it long' as well, but that was really just a variation of 'down the guts'.

Opposite me, on the wall, there was a sign in big black letters – 'WINNING ISN'T EVERYTHING IT'S THE ONLY THING.'

Winning. Losing. Winners. Losers. The old man went on about it all the time. 'There's only two types of people in the world, son – winners and losers. Now, which one do you wanna be?'

'Um, think I'd like to be a loser, Dad, if that's okay with you.'

There was a knock on the door. An umpy, all in white, appeared. 'You've got ten minutes,' he said in a high voice.

'Sit down, everybody,' said Arks.

Time for the pep talk.

We all squeezed along the bench, thigh against thigh. Arks stood in front of us. He bent over slightly from the waist so that his eyes were on the same level as ours. His slicked hair glistened under the lights. He was holding a footy in one hand.

'Youse lads,' he began. 'This is it.'

Thwack! He slammed the footy into his other hand.

'This is what we've been playing for all year.'

Thwack!

'The whole of the Port is here to watch youse today.'

Except my old man, I thought.

'And they ain't going home disappointed.'

What did I tell you – football breeds optimism.

Thwack!

'This ain't just a game of footy,' he said.

Yes it is, I thought, looking down at my boots. That's exactly what it is – just a game of footy. Just a stupid game of footy. Who cares if we win? Does it really matter? What does it prove? The Port will still be a dump. Arks's Pollywaffles will still be stale. The old man will still think I'm a gutless wonder. I looked up. It was quiet, absolutely quiet. Arks was looking right at me, his black eyes boring into mine.

'This ain't just a game of footy,' he repeated.

Arks was right – for him it wasn't just a game of footy. What he said was the truth, his truth anyway, even if it wasn't quite mine.

'Remember who you're playing for.'

He walked slowly along the line of players, still bent over.

'Your team.'

Thwack!

'Your town.'

Thwack!

'And the glory.'

Double thwack!

'The glory, lads. The glory of a premiership. Think of it, lads. The glory. No matter what ya do, for the rest of your life, they can never take it away from you.'

His voice was getting louder now, his face getting redder.

'So get out there and get that glory.'

Thwack!

We were all standing up now, pressing together, urging each other on.

'Come on, Deano!'

'You can do it, Dumby!'

'It's your day, Pickles!'

It's your day, Pickles?

Arks's pep talk was ridiculous, but it was impossible not to be affected by it. My heart was thumping in my chest. I was pumped up, charged with energy. We all were. I was ready to bound out onto the oval, grab the ball, stream down the field brushing off tackles like they were bushflies and drill the first goal of the game.

'One last thing,' said Arks as we were about to run out, 'and I've arksed youse this a million times. No buggerising around on them flanks. Up the guts every time you get that ball.'

We ran onto the field, except I can't remember actually running. It was like I was being swept along, carried along by something bigger and stronger than I was. Something awesome.

'Way to go, Robbo.'

'Up and at 'em, Clemboy!'

'Ya gunna murder him, Blacky!'

As we crossed the boundary line, horns started beeping, people started yelling. Then Wangaroo ran out and our supporters were swamped as an enormous wave of sound washed over the oval. Best Team-man was right, those magpies did barrack for Wangaroo, I could hear them screeching.

We were in position. I was ready to leap skywards, give the ball a mighty thump towards our goal posts. I looked across at my opponent. Huh! Only the Thumper. I was feeling sorry for him. Poor bastard. Imagine having to play against me on a day like this. The siren blew, the umpy bounced the ball. I watched it spinning in the air. Then I ran in and jumped, my arm outstretched. The first goal, the game and the glory would all be ours. I was high, high in the air, my fist almost touching the ball. The Thumper was nowhere to be seen. I'd out-jumped him, out-played him, out-smarted him. He couldn't do anything, just watch in awe as the best ruckman on the peninsula performed his football magic.

Ooof! A knee in the balls.

Ooof! An elbow in the face.

I tumbled out of the air, landing flat on my backside. The Thumper grabbed the ball, ran straight through three of our players (including Best Team-man) and kicked the first goal of the game.

The umpy bounced the ball again, I jumped again, I was flattened again, Wangaroo scored another goal. Again and again and again.

By quarter-time the game was pretty much all over. We huddled together like a mob of lost sheep. Nobody said anything, but I knew it was my fault. A footy game is won and lost in the ruck – a fact of life.

'Gary, Gary.'

It was my sister, Jenny. She was trying to squeeze between some of the players to get to me.

'Piss off, will ya?' I said.

It was bad enough to be the cause of your team's certain demise without being pestered by your little sister.

She wouldn't go away though. Arks launched into another pep talk.

'Go the guts, lads. Go the guts.'

As we broke up to go to our positions, Jenny followed after me.

'What the hell are you doing? Get off the oval!' I said.

'Mum says run in from the side and jump late.'

'What?'

'Off the oval please, young lady,' said the umpy in his squeaky voice.

'Run in from the side and jump late,' said Jenny as she ran towards the boundary.

From the side. Jump late. Arks wouldn't like it – not direct, not the guts. But things couldn't be any worse.

So that's what I did. I stopped running straight at the Thumper. I ran in from the side, and I jumped late. It worked, of course. Like I told you, my mum was a fair-dinkum tactical genius. Thumper stopped plucking the ball out of the air, Wangaroo stopped kicking goals at will. We started to score a few of our own. Dumby was on fire at half-forward, Mark Arks was playing well,

105

and bit by bit we made up the difference. At three-quarter-time we were dead level.

And that's how it stayed. Wangaroo kicked a goal. We kicked a goal. Wangaroo scored a point. We scored a point.

I looked up at the scoreboard clock – there was only time-on left, two or three minutes at the most. Mark Arks had the ball, he let fly with a huge torp. But it was too long. It went way over Deano's head and was headed straight for three Wangaroo players standing together. One of them was sure to mark it. But then I saw Dumby running up behind them. He was really moving, too. Then he jumped, his leg stuck out in front, climbing up on the back of one of the Wangaroo players.

Idiot, I thought. He's jumped too soon. The ball isn't anywhere near them.

But he kept climbing, higher and higher. I'd never seen anybody so high. Never. Not even Jezza in the 1970 final got that high. And Dumby stayed there, up in the air, way above those three Wangaroo players, like he was never going to come down. The only thing moving was the ball as it spiralled closer and closer until it landed in Dumby's outstretched hands. And then he fell out of the air, down, down, down, crashing into the ground.

'Ooooooh!' went the crowd.

Dumby jumped back up.

'Aaaaaah!' went the crowd.

Then everybody clapped. I mean everybody – even

the Wangaroo supporters. I knew why, too. They'd just seen the mark of their lives. They knew that no matter how many footy games they went to after that, how many replays they watched on the telly, how many books they read, they'd never see a better mark, a bigger speccy, than that one.

When the noise had died down Dumby slowly walked back. He pulled up his socks, did up his right bootlace, and ran his fingers through his hair. He plucked some grass from the ground and tossed it in the air. It fluttered to his feet – there was no wind. Then he lined up the goals. Dumby was the deadliest kick in our team, probably on the peninsula. He couldn't possibly miss from there. We all stood there and waited for him to stick it through the big white ones.

He ran in. Long, balanced strides. He kicked. There was a sweet sound as his boot connected with the ball.

I was looking at the goals, waiting for the ball to split the middle. The goal ump would raise those two fingers and the game (and the glory) would be ours.

Except the goal ump's fingers stayed exactly where they were. Instead the field ump blew his whistle. Clemboy had the ball. Dumby had passed it to him!

I couldn't blame Arks for yelling out what he did. I couldn't blame him for using that word in public, in front of little kids, and their mums, and grannies, and even two nuns. If I was the coach and the best kick in the team had passed the ball when he had a set shot from thirty metres out, straight in front, with a minute to go in the grand final, I probably would've used the eff-word, too. I think even the nuns understood.

Clemboy was maybe five yards closer to goal. But Clemboy wasn't the deadliest kick in the team, Dumby was. Clemboy wasn't the worst kick in the team, either. I was. But he was next.

He ran in with little stuttering steps and kicked. The ball ballooned off his foot and floated just to the left of the right-hand point post.

Only a point. But still, it was enough. All we had to do was stop Wangaroo from scoring a goal and we'd win.

The noise was incredible. The Wangaroo crowd was urging, urging, urging their players on. Our crowd was doing the same.

Arks was bellowing, 'Down the guts, down the guts.'

Tommy Red was yelling, 'Chug-a-lug, chug-a-lug.'

Shirl was screaming, 'C'mon Port, C'mon Port.'

There were maybe twenty, thirty seconds to go. The ball flew over my head. I jumped but it was too high, it brushed past my fingers and fell into the Thumper's massive arms. He looked up, checked where the goals were and started running. One bounce. Two bounces. I looked around, but I was the only one. Between Thumper and the goals, between Wangaroo and victory, was me. Mass of a stick insect.

All the other players stopped. There was nothing they could do but watch. This was between me and the Thumper.

Three bounces. Four bounces. He was getting closer and closer, bigger and bigger. He'd reached terminal velocity, full momentum.

There was a voice in my head.

It's just a game of footy, Blacky. The team, the town, the glory – that's all crap. What's important is your life. You've only got one of those. There'll be other grand finals, lots of them. If you try to stop the Thumper, you'll be killed. If not killed then crippled. Don't mess with momentum, Blacky. It maims.

It was good advice. I decided to do the Thumper tackle. Nobody would know the difference. We'd lose, but nobody would blame me.

'Shhtop that monshter!'

It was Shirl. I could see her out of the corner of my eye. Standing up. In her oversized footy jumper, those seagull legs sticking out. A stubby in her hand. She wanted me to stop that monster.

Fat chance, Shirl.

'Please, Blacky.'

It was Arks. His voice almost gone. It was a plea, a prayer. Please, Blacky. All those grand finals and not a bloody one. Please, Blacky.

Sorry, Arks. I'd like to. I really would. But let's face it – it's only a game after all.

Nobody was yelling now. Silence.

One more bounce and the Thumper had almost arrived. Head down. Legs, arms pumping like pistons. I could hear him breathing, sucking in great lungfuls of air.

I looked over towards the beer tent. There was a huge mob of blokes there, all crowded together. But I couldn't see the old man.

So I took a little sidestep to my right, to get out of the Thumper's way. But at that exact same second he veered to his left. I'd stepped right into his path. And by then it was too late.

And that's the last thing I remember.

When I came to I was lying on a bed. Mum was there. Best Team-man. Arks. Their faces huge and blurry.

'Am I okay?' I said.

'You're fine, dear,' said Mum.

'Not crippled?' I said.

'Just concussion,' said Arks, smiling.

What's he smiling for? I thought. I've almost been killed and Arks is smiling.

'That was a gutsy effort, Blacky. Tackling him like that,' he said.

What was Arks on about? I was trying to get out of the way, not tackle him.

'It was a very brave thing to do,' said Mum. 'We're all proud of you.'

'I stopped him, then?' I said.

'Not really,' said Best Team-man. 'He just ran straight through you. He still kicked a goal, you know.'

'But you slowed him down. The siren went. The goal didn't count,' said Arks.

'So we won?' I said.

'We surely did,' said Arks. 'We surely did.'

His face dissolved into a huge Luna Park smile as I slipped back into unconsciousness.

15

'Please, Mum, please can I go? Everybody else is.'

The rest of the family had already gone. The rest of the town had already gone. The only people at home were me and my mum.

'The doctor said you should rest.'

'But I feel okay. I really do.'

Which was a lie. I felt terrible. I'd heard people talk about splitting headaches. Now I knew what they meant. There was a nasty little man in my head, with a sledgehammer, driving a wedge deep into my brain. But I was determined to go, even if he came with me.

'You don't look okay. You're as white as a sheet.'

'But Mum, you'll waste your perm.'

The only time the ladies in our town got a perm

was when there was a Do – a wedding, the school speech night or something like tonight.

'Don't be silly.'

'But you will.'

I didn't know why they called it a perm, when it wasn't permanent. They should've called them temps.

'It won't last until the next Do.'

But I was on the wrong tack because my mother was the ultimate Best Team-man. Absolutely the first lemming off the cliff. I had to change course, talk about me, and not her.

'This'll probably be the only grand final I ever win.'

'There'll be plenty more,' she said.

'No there won't. What if I die tomorrow?'

'Don't be silly.'

'Plenty of kids my age die. Car accidents.'

I could see she wasn't budging. It was time to employ the heavy artillery.

'Shark attacks.'

Mum had this thing about sharks, she sat through *Jaws* with her eyes closed.

'There was that kid last year up the coast. Thigh-deep he was, and the shark just cruised in.'

I could see that this bothered her, the idea that her son could be gobbled up by a shark without ever having been to a premiership Do. I kept going.

'And bit him clean in two.'

'Okay, then,' she said. 'We can go. But promise me you'll take it easy. No gallivanting around.'

'I promise. No gallivanting.'

Whatever that was.

There was a bottle of the old man's Aspros in the bathroom cabinet. I ate two of them.

The Institute was a blaze of light. Everything else was closed, including the pub. The car park was full and there were cars parked on both sides of the main street, all the way to the jetty.

'Practically the whole town's here,' said Mum as we walked inside.

This was one of Mum's sayings. There'd be six old ladies and a black dog at a CWA fete and she'd come back saying that practically the whole town was there.

But tonight practically the whole town was there. There were people inside and outside. There were people sitting and people standing. There were babies, kids, grown-ups and grandparents. There were people I'd never seen before. There were people I thought had carked it years ago.

'I'd better go and help the other ladies get the plates ready,' said Mum. 'But remember what I said – no gallivanting.'

'I'll be okay, Mum.'

They'd really done the place up. Black and white everywhere. Black and white streamers looped around the walls, bunches of black and white balloons hanging from the ceiling, black and white crepe covering the tables. Along one wall ran an enormous banner. 'THE PRIDE OF THE PORT' it said.

'Over here, brudda!'

It was Dumby Red. He was sitting, along with the

rest of the team, at a table in the front of the stage.

'Hey everybody, Blacky's here,' said Dumby, and the other players turned around to look at me. They started clapping, yelling out stuff.

'Onya, Blacky.'

'Gutsy effort, Blacky.'

'Way to go, Blacky.'

I felt embarrassed. Like I was a fraud. I hadn't meant to stop the Thumper. It was a fluke.

'Didn't think you was coming,' said Dumby. 'But I bagsed you this chair just in case.'

I sat down. Dumby put his arm around my shoulder.

'How ya feelin'?' he said.

'Pretty average,' I said.

Which was the truth. The Aspros had helped a bit, but not that much. That nasty little man was still at it.

'Christ Almighty, did you go down or what? Like a sack o' shit. I thought you was dead.'

'So did I,' I said.

Arks was sitting at the end of the table. He'd been wrapped, like an Egyptian mummy, from neck to toe in black and white streamers, only his head sticking out. And what a happy head it was. At last, after eight grand finals and not a bloody one, the glory was finally his. It surrounded him. He swam in it like a fish. People were congratulating him, slapping him on the back.

'Good onya, Robbo. Just what this town needed.'

'Knew you'd get there one day, Robbo.'

People who didn't follow the footy, who never bought a ticket in the Friday-night chook raffle.

114

'A premiership sure is a wonderful thing,' said one of them.

'Brings a town together,' said another.

Then Arks noticed me. The happy head got even happier.

'Blacky,' it said, beaming. 'I love you.'

Now I was embarrassed. Totally.

'Come on, Dumby, let's go get a chop,' I said, standing up.

The barbie was out the back. Sizzling on the hotplate were rows and rows of plump sausages and a mass of fatty chops. In one corner there was a mountain of tangled onion. Next to it, on a table, were loaves of white bread and bottles of tomato sauce.

Standing behind all this, tongs in one hand, a beer in the other, was our local butcher, Slogs Kneebone. Slogs looked like mettwurst – he was fat and lumpy and his skin had the same greasy texture. Slogs smelt like mettwurst. Let's face it – Slogs was mettwurst.

I had this theory. Years ago, during a wild storm, a bolt of lightning struck a stick of mettwurst that was hanging in the butcher's. A remarkable metamorphosis took place – legs developed, arms developed, a head, of sorts, popped out. Slogs Kneebone was born.

He was wearing one of his humorous aprons (he had a whole collection of them) – 'PLEASED TO MEAT YOU' this one said.

'How ya going, champ?' he said when he saw me. He waved his tongs.

'What can I do ya for? Coupla snags? Nice juicy chop?'

'A chop, thanks,' I said. 'What about you, Dumby? You want something?'

'Nah, mate.'

Slogs handed me the chop. I took a bite. I knew it! When Slogs turned away, I threw the rest in the bin. I just couldn't eat anything he cooked. It always tasted like mettwurst to me. I liked mettwurst, when it was mettwurst. I didn't like it when it was a chop, however.

'You wanna drink?' said Dumby.

'Sure,' I said.

He came back with two Cokes.

We sat down.

'Can I ask ya something, Dumby?' I said.

'Sure, fire away.'

'Why'd you pass the ball for?'

'When?'

'You know, after you took that amazing mark. Did Clemboy call for it?'

'Not really.'

'Then why'd you pass it?'

'Dunno.'

'C'mon, you must've had a reason.'

'Cos Clemboy hadn't had a kick all day.'

'Cos he hadn't had a kick?'

'That's right, I didn't wanna see Clemboy shamed. He's me cousin, unna.'

'But, Dumby, according to you all the Nungas are your cousins.'

'That's right.'

'Christ, Dumby, I'll never understand you blackfellas.'

'And I'll never understand you whitefellas.'

We both laughed.

'Is that your old man over there?' said Dumby.

It was him all right. It was the first time I'd seen him that day. He was standing next to the keg with Mick and a couple of other front-bar regulars. He had a plastic cup of beer in each hand. He was laughing. Free piss always made him happy.

'Yeah, that's him,' I said.

'Wanna go over and see him?'

'Nuh, let's go. I'm still hungry.'

'Get yourself some tucker,' said Dumby as we walked back inside. 'I'll be over there.'

He pointed to a table where a group of girls was sitting, including a couple of my siblings. They started whispering and giggling when they saw Dumby coming.

At the back of the Institute were five or six trestle tables. They were loaded with food – I'd never seen so much. I took a plastic plate and started piling it on – a piece of cold chook, some tuna mornay, a sausage roll, some potato salad, half a mini-pizza.

The plate started to sag in the middle.

'Sure you got enough?'

It was Clarence, Dumby's sister. She was wearing a

Port footy jumper. And jeans. She had a white streamer, like a headband, tied around her head.

'Didn't think you'd make it,' she said. She had a plate in her hand with a lamington on it.

'Doctor reckons I got concussion.'

'No wonder, brudda. Standing in front of that monster.'

'You're not gunna eat that lammie are ya?' I said.

'Why? What's wrong with it?'

'It's one of old Mrs Porter's.'

'And what's wrong with it?'

'You know old Mrs Porter?'

'Nuh.'

'She's got dandruff. Really bad.'

Clarence looked down at her plate.

'Yuk!' she said. She put the lammie back on the table.

'Whatta you recommend then?'

'Those little pink lammies are Mrs Fraser's. They're okay, but she doesn't use real cream. Those big ones are Mrs Bedser's. We call 'em Mrs Bedser's Bricks. That's what they taste like, too. Dazza's mum made those ones there. They're pretty good. But I reckon you're better off with those, over there.'

'Who made 'em?'

'Me mum.'

Clarence laughed.

'Your mum got dandruff?' she said as she put two lammies on her plate.

'No way.'

'What about your mum?' I said. 'Is she here?'

'My mum?' she said, looking at me like I'd just asked a really dumb question.

'You know – your mum. Your mother. The woman who gave birth to you,' I said.

'Nuh, she ain't here. She's not keen on being 'round you lot.'

You lot? What did she mean by that? I felt a bit insulted.

'Why not?'

'Stop asking such tricky questions, will ya? She's just not. She's happy staying out the Point with our mob.'

Actually there weren't so many Nungas at the Do. Not when you considered that half our team was from the Point. I'd seen only one table inside, with maybe twenty people sitting at it. And there was a group of blokes near the keg.

Clarence's voice dropped.

'You smoke, Blacky?' she said. 'Wanna come out for a durrie?'

I wasn't much of a smoker. I'm not sure why. It wasn't because I was a goody-two-shoes or anything. I just didn't like it that much.

'Yeah, love to,' I said.

'Meet you outside in ten minutes.'

'Okay.'

16

'Hey, Blacky, over here.'

I looked around, but I couldn't see anybody. Then Clarence stepped out from behind the wall. She brought her hand out from behind her back. There was a cigarette, a tailor-made, sitting in her palm.

'Not here,' I said. 'Somebody might see us.'

'Where, then?'

'Down the jetty, it's not too far.'

'Okay, let's go then.'

As we walked off I thought I heard somebody snicker. I turned around.

But there was nobody.

'How many of youse Blackies anyway, Blacky?' said Clarence.

'Eight kids.'

'Big mob, unna? Just like us Nungas, too much courtin',' she said, smiling.

'Yeah,' I said, a little embarrassed.

But at least she hadn't said, 'Catholic then, are you?' like most people did.

There was a lone figure at the end of the jetty, under the lighthouse, standing in a pool of light. It had to be Darcy, of course. The only person in town not at the Do.

We walked along the railway lines. Clarence was really good at it. She didn't fall off, not once, not until we reached the shed. I'd never seen anybody do that, not even Deano, who reckoned he was so good at it he was going to join the circus and become a tightrope walker.

We sat down in the shed, on opposite seats.

'Mmmm, smells lovely in here,' said Clarence.

Like fish guts and cigarette smoke and stale beer.

The smell didn't really bother me, but something else did. Right above where Clarence was sitting was some graffiti. 'BOONGS PISS OFF' it said. It was written in enormous block letters. Even in the gloom the black paint stood out clearly against the white of the shed.

If you wrote something like 'MONICA IS A SLUT' then it wouldn't last very long, maybe a week, but 'BOONGS PISS OFF' had been there for ages. I didn't have a clue who wrote it, and I could recognise most people's writing.

I wasn't sure if Clarence had seen it; she didn't say

anything. Still, I didn't feel comfortable. I felt guilty in some way. I hadn't written it, but I hadn't scratched it out either.

'Sure does pong,' I said, holding my nose. 'Let's go under the jetty.'

'Suits me,' said Clarence.

There was only one way under the jetty, from the end, where old Darcy was fishing.

'Congratulations, young'un,' he said when he saw us coming. He didn't say anything to Clarence.

'Heard you done it, pulled off the big one. How's the Do going up there?'

'Pretty good. Just getting some fresh air. Caught anything?'

'Not a bloody thing. Not even a bloody bite.'

Clarence disappeared under the jetty.

'Been using the mutton gent. But I'm not having much luck with him. Time to change I reckon.'

He reeled his line in.

'Young Blacky, can I offer you a word of advice?'

He opened his bait box, an old artillery case, and took out a jar of gents. He unscrewed the lid, lifted the jar up to eye level, tilted it to one side and gave it a gentle shake.

'There's a beauty,' he said, picking out a maggot, holding it delicately, with thumb and forefinger. 'Just a word of advice from an old bugger who's seen a thing or two in his day. You be careful of these gins now, lad. Nice girls, but they've all got the clap. Every last one of 'em.'

He speared the maggot, fat and squirming, with the hook.

'Thanks, Darce,' I said, as I lowered myself, feet first, over the side.

Clarence was already there – under the jetty, astride a crossbeam, her back against a pylon. She was looking down, into the water, humming a tune. I knew the song – 'An Octopus's Garden'.

'Don't like that old fella. He your mate is he, Blacky?'

'S'pose. He's okay, minds his own business.'

'Does he now?'

'Whatta ya mean?'

But Clarence didn't reply.

I wondered what Darcy had meant – all gins have got the clap. Every last one of them. I remembered a film we'd seen at school, about a corroboree. The men stomping in the red sand, surrounded by women who were chanting and clapping sticks. Was this the clap he meant? Did it have some sort of magic power? Was it like pointing the bone? I looked over at Clarence as she lit the cigarette. She didn't look too scary. But old Darcy did know a thing or two. He was right, I better be careful.

I could see the tip glowing redder and redder. Christ, she was really dragging it in! She must've been smoking all her life.

Clarence blew a plume of smoke from the side of her mouth. She really knew how to smoke, all right. Probably blow smoke rings and all.

'Deadly,' she said, and passed me the durrie.

I took a drag. Was she watching? No, thank goodness, she was looking down at the water again. I blew
the smoke straight out, without taking it into my
lungs.

'Deadly,' I said, and passed the durrie back to
Clarence.

She'd started humming the same song again.

'That's a Beatles' song, isn't it?' I said.

'Surely is,' said Clarence. 'You like The Beatles,
Blacky?'

'Yeah, I do.'

'Deadly, unna,' said Clarence.

'Deadly, unna,' I agreed.

Then there was silence.

I never knew what to say to girls. With boys it was
easy, if you ran out of things to say you just insulted
them. Like 'Geez Pickles, you've got a head like a rob-
ber's dog'. You couldn't do that with a girl, though. Not
if you wanted to impress her. I wanted to impress
Clarence.

She took a drag. Then she tilted her head back. She
blew a smoke ring, then another, then another. Three
perfect circles drifted away from the jetty. Then the
wind caught them and pulled them apart. Wisps of
smoke floated upwards, into the night sky.

I racked my brain. What could I say? Then I remembered what Malcolm Prestwidge had told me.

'Clarence,' I said, 'did you know that some of those
stars you see up there are actually dead?'

She looked up. She took a while to answer.

124

'How can they be dead if you can see 'em?' she said.

I knew the answer.

'Because they're so far away, light years away, and it takes ages for their light to reach us.'

Clarence laughed.

But I continued, 'And by that time they're dead.'

'You sure have some funny ideas, Blacky.'

'It's not an idea. It's the truth.'

'The truth, eh? Then tell me – why do them stars die?'

'They burn out,' I said.

Clarence laughed again. She wasn't impressed. I could tell. Not at all. I felt like a complete dickhead.

'Shit!' I said, looking at my watch. 'Look at the time. We better get back. We'll miss the awards.'

Clarence flicked the ciggie. It tumbled, sparks flying off the end, like a tiny Catherine Wheel, into the sea.

17

When we got back Big Mac was already on the stage, stooped over the microphone. Big Mac was the president of our club. And the secretary (except that's not how he pronounced it, he said 'secatree'). He was also the local publican. Victor James McRae was his real name. It was written in gold letters above the pub's front door. But everybody called him Big Mac.

I had this theory (yes, another one). To be president of a footy club you needed to possess three qualities. Number one – you had to have a fair-sized gut. Number two – you had to sweat a lot. Number three – you had to breathe heavily, preferably through the nose.

Big Mac had been president of the footy club ever since I could remember. Elected unopposed.

He had the biggest gut in town, probably the

peninsula. He was sweating profusely under the lights, his nylon shirt sticking to his body. You could see the pink flesh of his chest covered in curly black hair.

He switched on the mike. The sound of his breathing boomed through the hall.

'Ladies and gentleman, boys and girls, distinguished guests. First I'd like to welcome youse all here tonight on this auspicious occasion. It's been a long time between drinks. Thirty-eight years since we last had a premiership in this town. A bloody long time, but I'm sure you'll all agree it's been worth the wait.'

Everybody cheered.

The hall was chockers now. All the seats were taken. In front of the stage kids were sitting on the floor, and the blokes were all standing at the back, drinking their free beers.

'And as president and secatree of the Port Football Club it is my great pleasure to introduce you to somebody who needs no introduction, somebody youse all know well, please give a warm welcome to the number one ticket holder of the Port Football Club, our local member, Mr Bernie Wilmott.'

The local member stood up. There was a smattering of applause.

The local member reminded me of Johnny Beelitz, this kid in my class at school, even though he didn't look anything like him. Johnny Beelitz was always the first to put his hand up when the teacher had a question. 'Please, Sir. Please, Sir. I know.' (Most of the time he didn't.) He wore his trousers really high. He had one of those ties on, made of the stretchy elastic. He was a champion dobber. And of course he always got belted up after school.

The local member gave the same long and boring speech he always gave. He talked about his exemplary track record. About the sterling qualities he brought to the job. About his vital concern for our collective welfare. He talked about everything, except football. The hall was starting to empty; the blokes were drifting back to the keg, kids were playing chasey.

'At the end of the day,' said the local member, and he paused.

'Come on, Bernie,' yelled Shirl from the back of the hall. 'Pull ya bloody finger out.'

'Yeah,' somebody else yelled, 'get on with the bloody thing.'

The local member looked stunned, like a rabbit caught in a spotlight. His eyes blinked.

'Um, er,' he said.

'Probably thinks it's School Speech Night,' said Pickles.

Then the local member looked over and saw the trophies on the table.

'The trophy. That's right, the trophy,' he said. 'It's my great pleasure,' he continued, 'to present the trophies for outstanding academic achievement.'

'Told ya,' said Pickles.

Big Mac whispered something into the local member's ear.

'As I was saying,' said the local member, 'it's my

esteemed pleasure to present the trophies for today's football game.'

'About bloody time,' yelled Shirl.

The local member ignored her.

'A game won in grand style by the Port Football Club.'

People cheered. The hall started to fill up again.

The local member was on a roll now, his voice growing in confidence.

'First I'd like to present a premiership medallion to each of these fine young men.'

There were more cheers.

We filed onto the stage, one at a time, and got a medallion and a clammy handshake from the local member. Pickles was looking very pleased with himself. I'm sure he thought that from now on, with that medallion round his neck, he'd be spending quality time down the bushes.

'Now for the individual trophies. The first trophy, donated by the Progress Association, is the Best Team-man award.'

Here we go, I thought. Best Team-man wins another Best Team-man trophy. Another little silver man in our lounge room. We'll have to buy a bigger telly just to fit them all on.

'And the winner is . . . Tim Black.'

Just as I thought. But why is everybody looking at me? What have I done? Then I realised, he'd said Gary, not Tim. It was me! I'd won the trophy. I'd won Best Team-man's Best Team-man trophy.

'But, but, but . . .' I said.

I wanted to tell them that I didn't really deserve the trophy, they'd made a mistake. I hadn't meant to stand in front of the galloping Thumper.

'No buts about it,' said Arks. 'Go on, Blacky, get up there.'

Dumby pulled me to my feet, and I walked onto the stage, everybody clapping madly.

It felt weird to be up there, standing in front of all those people, all of them looking at me. I could see Mum sitting at a table, her hands clasped together. Clarence was next to Claire, both of them were smiling. The deliriously happy head of Arks was beaming up at me. Dumby was giving me the double thumbs-up. Even Team-man didn't seem upset that I'd stolen his trophy.

Again I shook the local member's clammy hand. He handed me the trophy. It was lighter than it looked. The little silver man was taking an overhead mark. His head was a weird shape, like it'd been squashed.

I gave a speech. I thanked the Progress Association for donating the trophy. I thanked Arks for coaching the team. I thanked all my team-mates.

As I came off the stage I could see the old man standing at the back of the hall.

Slogs was next to him. He was still wearing his apron.

'Over here, young Blacky,' he said. 'Let's have a look at that trophy.'

I walked back through the crowd of people.

'Good onya,' said Slogsy. He shook my hand.

'He done well eh, Bob?' he said to the old man. 'He's a credit to ya.'

The old man's cheeks were red. Which always meant he'd had a few. But he was in a good mood; he had that loose look about him.

'He done real well,' he said.

How would he know? I thought, he wasn't even there. He finished off his beer and let the plastic cup drop to the floor.

'Let me shake your hand, son,' he said.

He took my hand. I could feel the rough calluses on his palm. Then he squeezed.

My old man believed in a firm handshake. According to him, if a handshake wasn't firm then you were probably dealing with a bludger, or a no-hoper, or maybe even a poofter.

'It was a gutsy effort,' he said, looking me in the eye, squeezing harder.

'Thanks,' I said.

Little bones in my hand were crunching.

'We'll get you out fishing soon,' he said.

'Great,' I said.

He squeezed even harder. Christ! Little tears were forming in the corner of my eyes.

Finally, he let go.

'Gotta get back to the table,' I said.

As I made my way back to the table people were slapping me on the back.

'Well done, Blacky.'

'Onya, Blacky.'

Maybe I wasn't such a fraud after all. I mean, everybody else at the ground thought I'd tackled the Thumper. I was the only one who didn't. How could all those people be wrong? Maybe I'd tackled him without realising it – subconsciously. That was it – I'd subconsciously tackled him. I was starting to feel pretty good about myself. A premiership. Best Team-man trophy. The old man was going to give me another chance. I sat down.

'Which brings me to the last of tonight's presentations,' boomed Big Mac. 'The McRae Medal for best on ground. Donated by Desmond McRae, mine host at the Port Hotel, for all your liquid refreshment needs.'

The big one. B.O.G. Best on ground. Big Mac handed the trophy to the local member.

'And the winner is . . .' he said

I elbowed Dumby in the ribs. The McRae Medal was his. He'd had twice as many kicks as anybody else. Taken heaps of marks, including the speccy of the century. He'd booted five goals, half our score. Dumby was a sure-fire odds-on cert. He was unbackable.

'Mark Robertson!'

At first I thought they'd made a mistake, or he'd made a mistake, that dickhead local member. And I was feeling a bit sorry for Mark Arks because he was jumping up and down and getting all excited. The poor bastard thought he'd won the McRae Medal.

Any second now, I thought, they'll announce who the real winner is.

But they didn't. Mark Arks really had won the McRae Medal.

The whole place went apeshit. You'd think he'd just won the Brownlow the way they carried on. And I thought footy was supposed to be a team game. They all clapped and cheered as he walked onto the stage. They all clapped and cheered as he got his medal. They all clapped and cheered as he made his stupid speech. Not me, though. I got angry.

I looked around for Dumby. He'd gone.

'Bullshit!' I said to Pickles.

'Whatta ya mean?' he said.

'Mark Arks getting B.O.G. It's bullshit. That's Dumby's trophy.'

'Give it a rest,' said Pickles.

I got angrier. I could feel it growing inside me, getting bigger and bigger, stronger and stronger, like a whirly-whirly spinning across a paddock.

And then that nasty little man with the sledge-hammer started up again, bang bang bang into my brain.

I had to get out of there. It felt like everybody was crowding in on me, suffocating me.

I got up from my seat and pushed through the crowd.

'Where ya going, Blacky?' somebody said, grabbing me by the elbow. 'The party's just starting.'

'Piss off,' I said, and I shrugged them off.

Outside the air was cool. I could smell the salt in it. I started running, away from the Institute, back down

133

the main street. When I got to the anchor I stopped, and lay down on the bench.

Mark Arks – what a joke! It just wasn't right. It wasn't fair. But what could I do?

Then I started thinking about this bloke on the telly the other night, a Buddhist monk. He was protesting about some war or something. So he set fire to himself. I'm not kidding. Right there on the six o'clock news he pours kero all over himself and then lights a match. Whoosh! Up he went.

I could do the same, couldn't I? Protest. Not by setting fire to myself. That was a bit over the top. I'd retire, that's what I'd do. Retire. Hang up my boots. Withdraw my services. Terminate my brief and not particularly glorious career.

I'd tell them why, too. Because you cheated Dumby out of his medal, you lousy bastards.

Then I realised I was still holding my Best Team-man trophy.

I stood up. My weight evenly balanced, eyes down. I lined up the goals – two piles of seaweed on the beach. I ran up, and kicked. Leg straight, toe pointed, follow through. The Best Team-man trophy went spinning through the air, the little silver man's squashed head glinting in the moonlight. It bisected the two piles of seaweed and landed in the sand with a soft thud. Not a bad kick to end my career, I thought. Not bad at all.

'Youse can stick your footy,' I screamed at the top of my voice, 'up your arse.'

And then, for the second time that day, I slipped into unconsciousness.

Yep, Mum was right – too much gallivanting.

SUMMER

18

Some people reckon summer starts the day school breaks up. Others reckon it's the first of December. According to old Darcy it was when the gars first went on the bite. But I had my own theory – summer started when I walked down the main street of the Port and the first three people I ran into all said, 'Hot enough for ya, is it?'

It was early in the morning, but already warm. The sky was blue and sparkling. The sea was blue and sparkling. The sort of day you always have at the Gold Coast. According to the ads anyway.

Big Mac was hosing down the footpath in front of the pub.

'Gidday, young Blacky,' he said. 'Hot enough for ya, is it?'

'Sure is,' I mumbled, hurrying past.

I walked past the garage. Rocker, the mechanic, was leaning against an oil drum, drinking a bottle of Coke. As usual he was wearing a greasy white t-shirt with a packet of ciggies tucked into his sleeve, tight jeans and boots with pointy toes. Rocker had tatts down both arms. They were hopeless. I reckon he'd done them himself with a pin and a bottle of ink. His burnt-orange Monaro, the hottest car in town, was up on the hoist.

'Hot enough for ya, is it eh?' he said.

Rocker was from Queensland, he said 'eh' after everything.

'Sure is,' I said.

Arks was standing outside his shop, putting out the Four 'n' Twenty pie sign. He was wearing a white singlet and shorts. There were little beads of sweat running across his forehead. Maybe this would be it, the start of summer. But I wasn't confident. Ever since the grand final, and that was months ago, Arks had been behaving strangely. He was always in a good mood, never grumpy like before. I didn't like it, it wasn't natural. And he'd become even more obsessed with football. He hardly ever talked about anything else, not even the weather, and in the Port everybody talked about the weather. Most of the time that's all they talked about.

He smiled when he saw me. I crossed my fingers.

'Hot enough for ya, champ?' he said, wiping his brow with a crumpled hanky.

Hooray! Summer had started.

'Thinking about playing you in forward line next season,' he continued.

'Great,' I said.

I hadn't told him about my protest, my decision to retire. I hadn't told anybody. After the Do some kid had turned up with my Best Team-man trophy. Said he found it on the beach. Was there a reward? he'd said. I told him to piss off. But the little silver man was now in the lounge room, on the mantelpiece, getting acquainted with all the others.

'Reckon you'll do well up there. We could work on your kicking over the summer.'

'I gotta go, Mr Robertson. I'll see ya later.'

'See ya, champ.'

Dazza and Pickles were sitting at the anchor. They were both wearing footy shorts and t-shirts. Dazza had thongs on. As usual Pickles was barefoot. He was cleaning his fingernails with his knife. It was a Buck, his pride and joy, and he kept it razor-sharp. There was a box, full of jars, in front of him.

'Gidday,' I said.

'Gidday,' said Dazza.

Pickles said nothing.

'What's in the jars?'

'Gents,' said Pickles.

'You buy 'em from Darcy?'

'Nuh.'

'Where'd you get 'em from, then?'

'None of your business.'

'From Skippy,' said Dazza.

'Skippy?'

'Yeah, you know,' said Dazza and he started singing, 'Skippy, Skippy, Skippy the dead kangaroo.'

'You're kidding?' I said.

'No mate, I'm not. Pickles here rides out the highway until he finds Skippy the dead kangaroo. Then he slits it open and scrapes the maggots out of its guts with that knife of his.'

'What for?'

'Whatta ya think? He's gunna go into business 'gainst old Darcy.'

Nobody had ever thought of going into business against Darcy. He had a monopoly on the gent market.

'You're kidding?' I said.

'Why not?' said Pickles. 'It's a free world. Nuffin special 'bout those arsey maggots any rate.'

Pickles and Darcy didn't get on. Pickles called him Arsey Darcy, sometimes to his face.

'Just maggots aren't they?' he continued. 'Arsey carries on like they've got pedigrees or somethink.'

'How much you flogging them for?'

'Hundred for a dollar.'

Half what Darcy charged. Maybe Pickles Mickle was on to something.

A white car pulled up. A late-model Ford. The roof-racks were piled high with gear. There were two people in the front seat, one in the back.

'Campers,' said Dazza. He made it sound like a dirty word.

We always called them campers. Not tourists, not

holiday-makers: campers. And we hated them. We hated them because they came from the city, and we didn't. We hated them because they could hang around in shopping centres, and go to the flicks whenever they wanted, and eat Maccas three times a day. We hated them because of all the presents they got for Christmas – push-bikes and fishing rods and snorkelling gear and spear-guns. We hated them because they stuffed up the fishing. Because they got in our way when we went squidding. Because they sat on our seat by the anchor. We hated them, and we couldn't wait until they arrived.

The driver's door opened. A man got out. He stretched, the way grown-ups do after a long drive. He was wearing a tennis shirt, tennis shorts, short white socks and tennis shoes. Only thing missing was the racquet. But he wouldn't be playing tennis, not in the Port anyway, because our courts were full of cracks, weeds sprouting up through them. Somebody had nicked the net, too. Maybe it was just his idea of casual.

'Hello boys,' said Mr Camper. 'Great day, isn't it?'

We all agreed it was a great day.

Then the back door opened. A girl got out. She was about our age, I suppose. She was about medium height, her long brown hair was tied back in a ponytail, and she had sunglasses on. She was wearing cut-off jeans, all frayed at the edges, and a short yellow top.

She walked past, her ponytail bouncing.

'What's this thing here for?' she said, leaning against the anchor.

'It's from a windjammer,' I said.

'What's that?'

'It's a big sailing ship. In the old days they'd come here to load up with wheat and that. Then they'd race to be the first back to England.'

'How fascinating,' she said. 'Where's the nearest McDonald's?'

'Adelaide,' said Pickles. 'Sucks, doesn't it?'

Mr Camper gave her a please-don't-interrupt-while-I'm-communicating-with-the-natives frown.

'You boys are obviously locals,' said Mr Camper. 'Could you tell us where the McDermott holiday home is?'

He had a strange way of talking, with full-stops and commas, like he was reading from a book. Then Mrs Camper wound down the passenger-side window. She had a perm and an encouraging smile.

'Turn right at the pub,' said Dazza. 'It's about a mile down the road on the left. It's a big place with a boat outside. Can't miss it. If you end up at the boat ramp you've gone too far.'

'You staying there?' I said.

'As a matter of fact we are. The McDermotts are good friends of ours. We'll be spending a couple of weeks with them,' said Mr Camper.

'Usually we go the Gold Coast,' said the girl, flicking her ponytail. 'Last year we went to Disneyland.'

'Well, not this year,' said Mr Camper. He sounded a little annoyed.

'I'm sure we'll find plenty here to keep us occupied,' he said, looking around. It took a while before he actually found anything. Then he saw the jetty. 'The fishing must be excellent.'

'They've been getting a few good-sized tommies,' I said.

That was a lie. They hadn't been catching anything lately, but I didn't want to disappoint them.

'What's a tommy?' asked the girl.

'A tommy ruff. A type of fish,' I said.

'If you're going fishing you'll need some gents,' said Pickles, pulling a jar from the box. 'Got some right here. Nice and fresh.'

'Gents?' said the girl. 'What are they? Give me a look.'

Pickles handed her the jar, a smirk on his face.

She unscrewed the lid. Then she pushed the sunglasses onto the top of her head. Her eyes were brown, like her hair. She peered inside.

I expected her to scream, or faint, the way girls are supposed to do when they look into a jar of squirming maggots.

'Oh, maggots,' she said, 'and you call them gents. That's so cute. Look at the little darlings. Aren't they sweet. Can we buy them, Daddy, please can we?'

'Cathy!' said Mrs Camper. The encouraging smile had disappeared. 'Give the jar back to the boy, please.'

So her name was Cathy. As in Catherine.

'Please, Daddy. Can we please buy them?'

'Not right now, honey. Maybe when we get settled. Come on, we better get going. The McDermotts are expecting us,' he said.

Cathy handed the jar back to Pickles. Mrs Camper wound her window back up.

'Thanks, boys. No doubt we'll be seeing you around,' said Mr Camper.

He got back into the car, and so did his daughter. As they drove off, she gave us a little wave from the back seat. I gave a little wave back.

'Wow!' said Dazza, 'she's a spunk, eh?'

'Not my type,' said Pickles. Pickles' type had blonde hair and big knockers.

'Whatta ya reckon, Blacky?'

I didn't say anything. I couldn't.

'I said whatta ya reckon, Blacky, she was spunky, eh?'

'I gotta go,' I said.

I walked home, in a daze.

19

'You look really funny,' said Greggy as I walked into the kitchen. He was spreading Vegemite on a piece of bread.

'Do I?'

'Yeah, sort of sick.'

'I've been smitten.'

Now I knew exactly how Opal felt. She'd been smitten by the dark stranger, Zac Heynes.

'By a mozzie?' said Greggy.

He sure was spreading that Vegemite on thick.

'No, a girl.'

'Yuk. Did it hurt?'

'Not yet.'

'I hope I never get smitten by a girl,' he said, folding the bread in two.

Then he screwed the lid back on the Vegemite, and put the knife in the sink. He was a tidy kid, Greggy, I'll give him that, but he had a lot to learn about life.

20

The McDermotts were rich, maybe not filthy rich, but still rich. They'd been coming to the Port for ages; their shack was one of the first ones here. We called it a shack but it was bigger and better than our houses. The correct term, I suppose, was holiday house.

You always knew when the Maccas arrived in town for the start of the holidays, you could hear them. They'd come charging down the main street, in the latest-model Statesman, with a huge boat behind, and Mr Mac would be leaning on the horn – beep, beep, beep all the way to the jetty.

Mr and Mrs Mac looked like Americans. I don't know why, they just did. They both had blond hair with lots of contours. And they wore gold jewellery. Mr Mac spent most of his time on his boat, churning up the gulf. While Mrs Mac would be out in the back yard, on a banana lounge, in a bikini, working on her tan.

They had two kids – Andrew, who was my age, and Craig, who was a year older. They had blond hair too. Which was lucky for them, because they were surfies. They wore board shorts all the time, they had surf-boards and they were always reading magazines like *Tracks* and *Ripcurl*. They did everything, except surf. Not in the Port anyway, because we had no waves. Didn't worry those Maccas though. Didn't worry the local girls either, they all thought the Maccas were drop-dead gorgeous. Even my own stupid sisters. Especially my own stupid sisters.

I have to admit, though, that those Maccas had the knack, they knew exactly what to say to girls. It was uncanny. I used to think that by hanging around with them, I'd learn a thing or two, I'd get better. No way. I was still as hopeless as ever. In the end I decided chatting up girls was like rolling your tongue – it was a genetic thing. Either you were born with it, like those Maccas, or you talked about dead stars, like me.

Another thing about those Maccas, they went to Kings College, in Adelaide. Christ, and didn't they go on about it. What a great place Kings was. How good the Kings' footy team was. How some famous cricketer or another had gone to Kings. All the wonderful things they got up to at Kings. Kings this. Kings that. It really gave me the shits. I couldn't understand it either. To get into college you had to be really brainy, but the

Maccas weren't brainy. They knew a lot about surfing (the theory, anyway) and chatting up girls, but that was about it. So how in the hell did they get into college? It had me beat.

To tell the truth I didn't like the Maccas that much. But every summer I used to hang around with them. So did Pickles. So did Dazza. We all did. Because somehow they made things happen. It's like in chemistry – you've got this test tube full of these amazing chemicals but there's nothing happening, no action, they're just sitting there looking at you. Then you add a catalyst. Straightaway – fizz! pop! whoosh! Well, those Maccas were catalysts. And if you didn't hang around with them, you missed out on half the fun.

Still, at the end of last holidays I'd made a promise.

'Blacky,' I said to myself. 'This summer you're not going to have anything to do with those Maccas. They're such phonies.'

But now I had to break that promise. I had no choice. I was smitten, and the girl who smote me was staying with the Maccas. It was no big deal, anyway. Breaking your own promises never is.

21

Pickles and me were sitting at the anchor.

It was a muggy night. There were campers every-where, out for an evening stroll, in their bright clothes and sunburned faces, eating ice-creams. Most of them were double-headers; they were loaded these campers.

'Did you see the Maccas today?' I said.

'Yeah. They were up the jetty with that chick. But I didn't talk to 'em much. Too busy with me gents.'

'What were they doing?'

Pickles gave me a funny look.

'Squirming around as usual,' he said.

I felt sick inside. The Maccas had been squirming around with Cathy. Up the jetty. In public.

'What, in front of everybody?'

'Sure.'

'You're kidding?'

'Maggots aren't exactly shy, you know.'

'The Maccas, not the maggots, you dickhead. What were the Maccas doing?'

'I dunno, just showing her 'round I s'pose.'

'Were they holding hands or anything?'

'You've got the hots for that chick, haven't you?'

'No way.'

'Then why you asking so many questions for?'

'You know me. I always ask heaps of questions. It's me nature.'

Pickles farted.

'And that's mine,' he said.

I shuffled to the end of the bench.

'Well, were they holding hands or not?'

'Not.'

Thank God for that.

'Wanna go over the pub, play a few games of eight-ball?' asked Pickles.

'I'm broke.'

'Don't worry,' he said, patting his top pocket, 'I'm loaded. Them gents went like hot cakes.'

'I dunno. I might just hang around here a bit.'

'She won't be coming down, you know.'

'Who?'

'That chick, what's-her-name.'

'How many times do I have to tell you? I'm not interested in her.'

'Like hell. Come on.'

'Okay, then. Let's go.' We strolled across to the pub.

22

Pickles pushed open the door. I followed. Inside it smelled like stale beer and cigarette smoke. The front bar was long and narrow. It had a tiled floor with a little gutter around the edge. Mounted on one wall was a set of shark's jaws. They were huge. Mick reckoned the shark must've been at least a fourteen-footer. Somebody had stuck a cigarette onto the lower jaw.

Old Froggy was hunched up in the corner, mumbling into his beer. Next to him a couple of dusty farmers were talking to each other, slowly squeezing out words. The regulars – the old man, Mick, Slogs and Rocker – were all standing at the bar. Shirl was sitting on a bar-stool, her legs crossed and an ashtray balanced on her knee. At the other end of the bar, two campers, wearing Bermuda shorts and long white socks, were playing eight-ball. Big Mac was standing behind the bar. His belt was undone and his hand was down his trousers. He was adjusting. A lot of blokes in our town did this. When we went to Adelaide I was always on the lookout, to see if city people did it as much. But they didn't – the only people I saw adjusting in the city looked suspiciously like country folk down for the Christmas shopping, or the Easter Show. I reckon it had do with beer guts. If you had one then you had two options. Either you slung your belt low, below the gut, the crotch at knee level and the bottom of your trousers all bunched up on your shoes. Or you pulled them right up, the belt riding high on your gut, trouser bottoms flapping in the breeze and plenty of sock on display. If you went for this option, as Big Mac did, then the crotch of your trousers would apply pressure to your reproductive organs. To relieve this pressure you'd always be adjusting.

'I gotta have a piss,' said Pickles. He went to the toilet.

'Christ, Bob,' said Big Mac to the old man when he saw me. 'That lad of yours don't stop growing.'

'Must be using the right fertiliser, eh?' said Rocker.

The farmers stopped squeezing words and turned around. Farmers love talking about fertiliser. Superphosphate is their favourite topic of conversation.

'He'll be top ruck on the peninsula next year, no worries,' said Slogs.

The farmers turned back to their beers.

The old man was smiling, looking almost proud.

Since the grand final his attitude to me had changed. He didn't ignore me all the time. I wasn't about to rush out and nominate him for Father Of the Year, but still, it was an improvement on the 'my own son a gutless fucking wonder' days.

'I was the same at his age,' said the old man. 'Grew two inches one year.'

'He'll be chasing the girls soon. Won't ya, luv?' said Shirl.

Which got me thinking about that camper again. Cathy. Cathy the camper.

Pickles returned.

'Coupla sarses for the boys,' said Mick.

'And some chips, too,' said the old man.

Big Mac grabbed two glasses from the tray.

'Mac,' came a voice from the other side of the bar, 'any chance of gettin' a beer over 'ere?'

The owner of the voice was standing at a small serving area, like a window. He was in the back bar, or the black bar as everybody called it, because that's where the Nungas did their groggin'.

'Hold your horses,' said Big Mac, as he poured our drinks. 'I'm busy 'ere.'

'How's your mum?' said Shirl. She stubbed out her ciggie.

'She's good,' I said.

'I don't know why Bob doesn't bring her down here. Give her a night out.'

Yeah, sure, Shirl. I could just imagine my mum sitting in the front bar, admiring the shark's jaws. Once a year, usually New Year's Eve, she'd put some lippie on and come down to the pub. But she'd sit in the lounge bar, with some of the other ladies, and sip a crème de menthe. The lounge bar was posh, or it was supposed to be. It had tables and chairs, even carpet with roses all over it (though it was old and threadbare and scarred with cigarette burns).

I took a sip from my drink. Big Mac sure made a top sars, I'll give him that.

'Another round for you blokes?' said Big Mac to the campers.

'No, not for us. We'll be off,' one of them replied.

'You boys keen on a game of eight-ball?' said Rocker. 'Me and Slogs'll take youse on.'

'Yeah, sure,' said Pickles.

I rushed over to get the good cue.

Pickles and I were a pretty good team. He was a better shot than me, especially the long ones, but I was good on tactics – which ball to play, where to leave the white, when to play dirty, that sort of stuff. And Pickles used to listen to what I had to say – about the only time he ever did.

'Heads or tails,' said Rocker, flipping a coin.

'Heads,' I said.

'Heads it is.'

'Mugs away,' I said.

'Mugs away' was one of the old man's sayings. And now I was saying it, without really thinking about it. It's crazy, isn't it, the stuff you sort of absorb from your parents?

Rocker was a good player, probably the best in the pub. And the more beer he drank the better he got. Slogs was hopeless, sober or drunk.

First game was close, only the black was left on the table. Rocker was lining up to sink it.

The phone rang.

'Rocker, it's the missus,' yelled Mac.

He was holding the phone an arm's length away from his ear, like he was getting a blast. This got a laugh from the regulars. It always did.

'For Chrissakes,' said Rocker. 'Can't she see I'm on the black? Tell her I'm on me way, eh.'

Rocker had problems with the missus. Big problems. She didn't like him staying down the pub sinking beers and playing eight-ball while she sat at home looking after the three little Rockers. She was always ringing up. Sometimes she came down the pub to try and drag him home. Once night she even threw her wedding ring off the end of the jetty. I went diving for it the next day and found it next to an abalone. Rocker gave me ten bucks and a ride in his burnt-orange Monaro. The missus didn't seem that pleased to get the ring back, though.

It was an easy shot, but Rocker missed.

'Shit!' he said, then he went to answer the phone.

It was Pickles's turn.

'Not too hard,' I said.

Pickles wasn't a bad player, he had a good eye, but he would've been heaps better if he didn't hit the ball so hard. Sure it looked great when it came off; the ball would thump into the pocket. But if he missed, the ball would ricochet madly around the table, knocking the other balls out of position, mucking up my carefully thought out strategy.

This time he curbed his ball-shattering impulse; the eight-ball dropped softly into the pocket. We won.

Rocker returned with two beers. He passed one to Slogsy.

'Rack 'em up, eh,' he said, handing me the money.

'Thought you'd be on your way home,' said Slogs, a smug look on his face.

Slogs was pretty pleased with himself. He wasn't married. (Who'd want to marry a greasy lump of mettwurst?) There was nobody ringing up, bothering him down the pub.

'Got time for one more, eh,' said Rocker.

Eight games, eight beers, and three phone calls later, he was still there.

By that time the farmers had gone. Old Froggy was still on the same beer, still mumbling away. The old man was getting pretty animated – he was doing his mad laugh – half kookaburra, half banshee. And didn't they love that down the front bar? Mick looked the same as always, beanie askew, rollie dangling from his lip. The ashtray on Shirl's knee was full of butts. Her stool was starting to wobble a bit. Every now and then she'd put out a steadying hand. In between pulling beers, Big Mac adjusted.

The front door swung open.

'Chug-a-lug, chug-a-lug.'

It was Tommy Red, Dumby's father. Since the grand final he'd been a frequent visitor to the front bar. He was wearing his cowboy hat, and those white shoes. He started shaking hands with the regulars.

'Gidday, Tommy.'

'How ya going, Tommy?'

'You're looking fighting fit, Tommy.'

Everybody liked Tommy. He was a real character.

'Ow ya going, champ?' he said to me, slapping me on the back. 'Chug-a-lug. Chug-a-lug. Can I get ya a drink? Mac, a raspberry for young Blacky 'ere. And young Mick, too. How ya going, young Mick? Orright? Chug-a-lug. Chug-a-lug. That's two raspberries, Mac. And some chips for the boys, too.'

And then Tommy started on one of his stories. About the time he'd rowed across to the island with a school teacher from Adelaide. They got caught in a storm and had to spend the night in a cave. Tommy really could tell a story, he had the knack. When you thought about it, what he was talking about wasn't that interesting. It was the way Tommy told it. His delivery.

Soon everybody was pissing themselves. Shirl almost fell off her stool. Even Mick had a smile on his face. Not Big Mac though. He was cleaning glasses, breathing heavy. Doing his Darth Vader impersonation.

Then there came some thumping noises from the black bar, like furniture was being thrown about.

'Bugger me,' said Tommy. 'Sounds like the bruddas having themselves a corroboree. Better get over then and sort 'em out.'

160

'Good onya, Tommy.'

'Catch ya later, Tommy.'

'Chug-a-lug. Chug-a-lug,' said Tommy.

'He's a character ain't he, that Tommy Red?' said the old man, when he'd gone.

'He sure is,' said Slogs. 'Pity there's not more like him out there.'

'Hey,' said Big Mac. 'Did ya hear the one about the boong and the priest?'

Everybody'd heard the one about the boong and the priest. But Big Mac started to tell it anyway.

'Hey, Mac, man's not a camel.'

There was somebody at the window.

'I'll be there directly,' yelled Mac. He continued with the joke.

'And the priest says to the truckie, don't worry I got the black bastard with the door!'

Big Mac burst out laughing, his big gut wobbling like a jelly on a plate.

And then he repeated the punch line, just in case we'd missed it.

'And the priest says I got the black bastard with the door!'

And they all laughed, all the regulars. Especially Slogsy. But I didn't. I don't know why, I'd laughed at the joke before. I'd even told the joke before. But tonight it didn't seem so funny any more. And I knew it had to do with Dumby and Clarence and Tommy.

23

I woke up. The kookaburra was at it again. I could see the blue sky through the window. Another hot and sunny day.

Then I remembered – I was smitten. Totally. I had to get up the jetty and see her. She'd be up there with the Maccas, for sure.

I scoffed breakfast. It was ridiculous, when you think about it. I'd seen her for ten minutes at the most, and for some of that time she was holding a jar of squirmy maggots. But still, there was no denying it, I was gone. Well and truly.

But then Mum had some jobs for me, so I was late getting there. The jetty was already crowded. A mob of kids was splashing around the shallow end – Learn To Swim classes. Mrs Matt, the teacher, was standing waist-high in water, a big straw hat on her head.

'Heads under the water, children,' she said, 'and let's all blow lots of bubbles.'

The kids all stuck their heads under, except Dazza's little brother.

'But the water hurts my eyes,' he said.

What a whinger.

Mrs Matt had taught just about everybody in the town how to swim, including me. Geez, those were the days. Head under. Lots of bubbles. Life was simpler then, that's for sure.

All along the jetty campers were fishing.

One of them pulled in a double header. Two fair-sized gars.

'Mind if I ask what bait ya using?' said the camper next to him.

'Not at all, mate. Gents.'

'That's funny, so am I and I haven't had a bite all morning.'

'Where'd you buy 'em?'

'From the boy, the scruffy lookin' one.'

'Well, that's your problem, mate. You gotta get yourself some of the Darcy gents. Swear by 'em, I do.'

When I got to the shed I stopped. I could see them all, lying in a line along the jetty, soaking up the morning sun, like lizards on a warm rock. First the locals – Pickles, Mark Arks, Deano and Dazza, all in footy shorts. Then the two Maccas in board shorts, reading surf mags. And next to them Cathy, in a bikini. It was yellow with white around the edges.

My heart skipped a beat, my legs turned to jelly, my insides went icy-cold – all that stuff in M&Bs that I didn't really believe, well, it happened to me. It was too much, I turned around to go back. But Pickles saw me.

'Blacky,' he said. 'Over here.'

So I kept walking.

'Hi, everybody,' I said. 'Great day, eh?'

Yeah, it was a great day, everybody agreed, except for Cathy – she didn't say anything. She was lying on her back, wearing those sunglasses. Her hair was in a plait. There was a brown bottle next to her head. 'Tropical Island Deep Tanning Oil' the label said.

I had two choices – either I put my towel down next to Pickles, or next to Cathy at the other end. What did he do, our brave hero? Yep, you guessed it. The towel went down next to Pickles.

'Geez,' said Pickles. 'D'ya have to put your towel so close?'

I wanted to get as close as possible to Cathy, without getting close to Cathy.

'You wanna root me or something?' he said.

'I don't actually,' I said. I lay down.

I stayed like that all morning. I didn't go with the others when they went to bomb the campers. I didn't go with the others when they went to dive off the lighthouse. I didn't go with the others when they went to have a fag under the jetty. I stayed there and watched her. Surreptitiously, of course. I wasn't perving or anything.

Every now and then she'd turn over. The front. The

back. Then the front again. Or she'd rub Tropical Island Deep Tanning Oil onto her skin. Occasionally she'd go for a swim. She'd dive off the second or third step (a neat dive, not much splash), and do a few strokes of freestyle (she was a good swimmer). When she came back she always squeezed the water out of her hair by twisting her plait. It was amazing how much it absorbed.

She didn't talk much. Sometimes her and the nearest Macca would have a whispered conversation. I could hear her giggling and I could feel the jealousy creeping around inside me like an octopus.

Or she'd just say something out loud and one of us would answer. Never me, though.

'Where's the sun gone?'

'Behind a big cloud.' (Deano.)

'How can you live in this dump without a McDonald's?'

'Sucks, doesn't it?' (Pickles.)

'Why do you guys always wear footy shorts?'

'Dunno.' (Mark Arks.)

But it didn't really matter what she said, or what she did – it was perfect. She was perfect, absolute perfection. By the end of that week I was more smitten than ever, smitten to the power of two. I couldn't stop thinking about her. It was like some alien had colonised my body and was controlling my thought processes. Stop thinking about her, I'd tell myself. And of course, I thought about her even more.

Was I miserable, or what?

24

Old Darcy was in his usual possie, at the end of the jetty, sitting on his bait box, his rod leaning against his leg.

'Gidday, young'un,' he said.

'Gidday, Darcy. How's the fishing?' I said.

I sat down next to him, my legs dangling over the side.

'Nothing doing early. But the tide just turned and that stirred 'em up. Just caught me a couple o' good size tommies.'

He tilted the bucket towards me so I could see them. They were opening and closing their mouths. I wonder what it feels like, I thought, drowning in air.

'One more for a feed, eh?' I said.

I don't know why but you needed at least three fish

before you could say, 'I got me a feed of tommies.'

'What bait you using?'

'Been doing a bit of experimenting,' said Darcy, handing me the jar.

'I started this lot off on the meat, nice bucket of pig guts I got offa Porky Fraser. Let the blowies strike that. Then when they got a bit of size to 'em, I put 'em on the fruit to fatten 'em up.'

Maggots weren't exactly my cup of tea, but I couldn't help but admire Darcy. He was always thinking, devising new strategies in his quest for the perfect gent.

'How they going?'

'Well, young'un, this is the first time I used 'em . . .'

He was interrupted by the whirr of the ratchet. He leaned back a little, and started winding the line in, the tip of the rod bending right over. A flash of silver, and Darcy had himself a feed of tommies.

'And as you can see they're not doing too badly.'

'Did you know Pickles is selling gents? He got them from a dead roo on the side of the road.'

I felt a bit like a traitor, because the night before I'd played eight-ball with money from Skippy the dead kangaroo's gents.

'Is that so? I had a notion that's where they were coming from. Don't worry, young'un. It's not the first time it's happened, and it won't be the last. But let me tell you something.'

His voice dropped, just like when he was reciting 'Kaiser Bill'.

'Nothing'll bite on filth like that. Nothing.'

We sat there for a while not saying anything. The waves lapping against the pylons.

'Darcy,' I said. 'Were you ever married?'

I didn't know much about Darcy's past, except that he'd been in the air force. He didn't have any kids, or if he did he never mentioned them, and they never visited him.

'Many years ago, young'un. Many years ago.'

'What happened?'

'Didn't work out. Nobody's fault, young'un. Just didn't work out. And I never got 'round to it again.'

'Do you wish you did?'

'Tell you the truth, young'un, I don't. I got nothing against sheilas, but I never understood them too well. Spent too much time by myself, I reckon. Got used to my own company.'

The ratchet whirred again. Darcy pulled in another one. Now he had a good feed.

'But I have got one piece of advice for you, young'un,' said Darcy as he cast again. A gentle flick of his wrist and the line went coiling through the air. 'As I can see you're in a bit of a state, and I know you're a shy sort of lad.'

Was I a shy sort of lad? Yeah, Darcy was right, I probably was.

'They're not mind-readers, you know. No use moping around with a long face. That's not telling her anything. If you like a girl then you gotta let her know. Maybe you'll make a fool of yourself. So what?'

Darcy turned his head so that he was looking me in the eye.

'Because I tell you something, young'un. You're a long time dead, a bloody long time dead.'

25

I walk along the jetty, with a spring in my step, towel slung over my shoulder, whistling a happy tune.

The gang are in their usual positions.

'Good morning, Mark. Pickles. Dazza. Deano. Morning Maccas,' I say, the words leaping from my mouth like super-heroes. 'A wonderful day is it not?'

'Sure is, Blacky,' they reply in unison.

'Morning, Cathy,' I say. 'Your tan's coming along great. Mind if I put my towel here?'

'Not at all,' she says.

I put my towel down, close to hers. Then I peel off my t-shirt and lie down.

Cathy turns to face me. I'm looking right into her sparky brown eyes.

'It took you long enough,' she says.

'It did, didn't it?'

She smiles, her teeth flashing white, leans over, and kisses me on the cheek.

That's how I'd envisaged it, anyway. I'd written my very own M&B, in my head. I called it *Love Story* (catchy title, eh?). I'd gone through it I don't know how many times since that talk with Darcy. The details varied, but the plot was always the same – up the jetty, me putting my towel next to hers, the smile, the kiss.

And today, I'd decided, was the day. Fiction was going to become fact. *Love Story* would become my story. There was no use moping about with a long face. Darcy was right about that. And my face was definitely getting longer. I'd been checking it out in the mirror. Every day longer and longer. I had to put a stop to it. Darcy was right about something else as well – you're a long time dead. The best time to put my towel down next to Cathy's was today, while I was still alive and kicking.

'Wanna go spearing today?' asked Team-man at breakfast.

I didn't reply. *Love Story* was playing in my head.

'Hey you,' he said, clicking his fingers in front of my face, 'I said do you wanna come spear fishing?'

'Spear fishing?'

'That's right, spear fishing. You know, with a spear. One of those long pointy things. We used to do it all the time, remember? You used to like it, remember?'

'No, no I don't think so. Not today.'

'Why not?'

'I've got something on.'

'What?'

'Just something, okay.'

'It's that camper, isn't it?'

'What camper?'

'What's-her-name. The stuck-up one.'

'It's not her, and she's not stuck-up.'

'Pathetic,' said Team-man. 'By the way, have you seen my thongs?'

'What thongs?'

'You know, my black ones.'

'No, haven't see 'em.'

'You sure?'

'Course I'm sure. I said so, didn't I? What would I do with your stinking thongs anyway?'

'Okay, just asking.'

I scoffed the last of my Weetbix. It was time to get ready.

Usually I didn't care what I wore, especially up the jetty; I just threw on whatever was around. But not today, today was different.

I got Team-man's thongs out from where I'd hidden them. They were too small for me, but they were black. Black thongs were hard to find, they were a definite fashion statement. And after a good scrub with Dettol the smell had pretty much gone.

Then I put on footy shorts. I'd thought about not wearing them, because Cathy had made a couple of snide comments about us locals wearing footy shorts all the time. But these were my lucky shorts; they were the ones I wore during the grand final. Besides, I was a local, and locals wore footy shorts swimming. Yet another fact of life. There was no getting away from it.

I had three t-shirts to choose from. The black, I decided, made me look too much like a hoon. I liked the white because it had squid ink all over it and I thought the stains made interesting patterns. I wasn't sure if Cathy would, though. So in the end I wore the blue.

I looked in the mirror. Not too bad, not too bad at all. I smiled. The severe occipital occlusion was still there, but everything else was looking good. I was ready.

Up the jetty I went. Past Mrs Matt, waist-deep in water, that big straw hat on her head.

'Heads right under, blow those bubbles,' she was saying.

Straight past the shed, the spring still in my step. The gang was there, in the usual spot.

I cleared my throat.

Are you ready, words? Are you ready to leap out and perform heroic acts?

'Good morning,' I said, but that was it, the rest of the words refused to budge. And even those two were pretty puny, like Superman after he'd been kryptonited.

Mark Arks grunted. There were no other replies.

Keep going, I told myself. And I did. Past Mark Arks. Pickles. Dazza. Past the Maccas. Until I was standing next to Cathy.

She was lying on her stomach, her back glistening

in the sun. And her hair, in a plait, curled around her neck.

I could hear Darcy's croaky voice, 'You're a long time dead young'un. A bloody long time dead.'

All I had to do was put my towel down. I'd rehearsed it a thousand times in my mind.

Go on, Blacky!

I slid the towel from around my neck. Just then the sun went behind a cloud, the only cloud in the sky that day.

Cathy stirred. 'Where's the sun gone?' she asked.

I panicked. I don't know why, but I did. I spun around and started walking, past the Maccas, past the others.

'Where you going, Blacky?' said Pickles.

'Forgot something,' I said over my shoulder.

Past the shed. All the campers. Mrs Matt and Learn To Swim. By the time I got to the start of the jetty I was running. Faster and faster. Black thongs flapping, my heels scrubbing on the road. All the way home. Into my bedroom and up onto my bunk. I buried my head in my pillow.

The old man's right, I said to myself, I'm gutless. A gutless fucking wonder. Tears were sliding down my face. They were salty, like the sea.

26

The next day I stayed away from the jetty. I went snorkelling with the siblings down at Bum Rock instead.

Floating about on the surface, the warm sun above, the cool sea below, watching the fish darting in and out of the weedy rocks, I realised I'd been a total idiot. Teamman was right. Cathy was stuck-up, of course she was, a typical stuck-up college girl. As phoney as those Maccas, if not phonier. And Pickles was right too, she wasn't even good looking. What a lucky escape, I thought to myself – I'd almost put my towel down next to hers. Imagine being stuck with her all summer, when there were so many other girls around. Girls who weren't stuck-up or phoney. Girls who didn't go to college.

As Pickles always said, 'Mate, it's a smorgasbord out there.'

Late that afternoon the weather changed. I could see it on the news, a big low rolling across the Nullarbor. The temperature dropped, the sky clouded over and the sea became choppy.

'Seen a couple of squid up the jetty this arvo,' said Darcy over the fence. 'You wanna get up there tomorrow with your jig.'

'Thanks, Darcy,' I said.

Go squidding. What a great idea! It was perfect squidding weather.

But I didn't want to go by myself. I had two choices – I could go with Pickles or Dazza. Dazza didn't fart all the time. He didn't spend all day scratching his filthy munga. He didn't have a hyperactive sexual imagination. Dazza was good company.

I dialled the number.

'Pickles, you wanna come squidding tomorrow?

But Dazza wasn't the best squidder in town. Pickles was. By a mile. He could do things with squid that would send a shiver up your spine.

'Wouldn't mind. Me gents have gone slack.'

So word had got out. I thought it would. Those campers were always talking to each other in the shower block. And what they were saying was – 'Just quietly, stick with the Darcy gent.'

'Let's go squidding then.'

'Okay. I'll meet you at the shed at seven.'

I woke early, before anybody else, and made myself breakfast.

Mum walked into the kitchen. She still had her dressing-gown on.

'You're up early, dear,' she said.

'I'm going squiddin'.'

She walked around the table so she could get a better look at me.

'Not in those clothes you're not,' she said.

'But they're old,' I said.

'I don't care if they're old, they're not covered in squid ink.'

Squid ink is real strong stuff. In the old days they used it for writing. Dipped their quills in it and away they went. If you got it on your clothes it didn't come off. Whenever one of those ads came on the telly about OMO or Drive or any other of those soap powders that were guaranteed to remove any stain (no matter how stubborn), my mum would say, 'They don't mention squid ink, do they? No, they don't, and I can tell you why; nothing gets squid ink out of clothes. Nothing.' She was right, too.

So the first thing you learnt about squidding was how to land the squid so the ink didn't end up all over you. (And the second thing you learnt was how to land the squid so the ink ended up all over somebody else, preferably a camper.)

I changed into my squiddy white t-shirt and some squiddy shorts. Then I got my lines, slocks, we called them, and a bag of tommy ruffs from the freezer for bait, and set off for the jetty.

Actually I was feeling pretty good. I was off squidding. And I was no longer smitten. That was all in the past.

Pickles was the only person on the jetty. He was sitting in the shed, sucking on a family-sized bottle of Coke.

'Brekkie,' he said, wiping his mouth with the back of his hand.

We put the slocks out, one at each pylon, all the way along the jetty. Then we sat down in the shed. Pickles started carving his name into the seat with his knife.

'BOONGS PISS OFF' was still there. Seeing it reminded me of the night of the grand final Do. I hadn't seen Clarence since then. Dumby either. I was having second thoughts about my retirement. What would I do if I didn't play footy? There wasn't anything to do in winter. And maybe I'd been wrong about the McRae Medal. Mark Arks had played really well. And that pass of Dumby's was lunacy.

Then Pickles farted. You can't imagine how bad a Pickles fart was. Take the worst fart you've ever experienced. Multiply it by ten thousand. Now you're getting close.

'Geez, Pickles, did you have to?' I said, holding my nose.

'Actually I did.'

I suppose he was right. It was his nature. You couldn't tell Pickles not to fart, it would be like telling a vampire not to suck blood.

'I'm going to check the slocks,' I said.

All the floats were bobbing high on the waves. Except for the one right at the end of the jetty. It was under the water. There was a squid on it.

I started pulling the line in. The float popped up. The squid had let go. I released the line. The float went under again.

Then I heard soft footsteps behind me.

A typical Pickles trick, he'd sneak up behind you, then drop his guts.

'I know you're there, you little piece of shit. Fair dinkum, if you fart, I'm gunna shove the first squid we catch fair up your arse.'

'My farts aren't that bad. Honest.'

Oh my God!

I turned around. It was her, Cathy. In jeans and a woolly white jumper. I'd never been so embarrassed. My face, I'm sure, was redder than Arks's had ever been.

'I'm sorry. I really am. I thought you was you. I mean, I didn't thought ... I didn't think you was you ... you were you. I thought you were Pickles.'

'That's okay,' she said, smiling.

'What are you doing up here, anyway?' I said.

'Early morning walk,' she said. 'Get out of the house.'

'Without the Maccas?'

'I *am* allowed out without them, you know,' she said. 'What are you doing – catching fish?'

'No, catching squid.'

'Really, catching squids.'

'Catching squid actually, because squid are like sheep, you know.'

'Squid are like sheep?'

'Because you don't have sheeps, do you? Same with squid. One sheep. Two sheep. One squid. Two squid and so on.'

'I see,' said Cathy.

I don't think she did actually and I couldn't blame her, my tongue was as tangled as those fishing lines on the old man's boat.

'Have you got one on?' she said, stepping closer to the edge, and looking over into the water.

'I have actually, but it's really touchy.'

'Touchy? What's that?'

I had to think about it for a while.

'It's suspicious. It doesn't trust me. Every time I start pulling the line it lets go.'

'Why?'

'I dunno, it knows something fishy's going on.'

Cathy laughed.

Was she laughing at me? My squiddy clothes? My tangled tongue? My severe occipital occlusion?

'What's so funny?'

'You made a joke – something fishy going on.'

'Oh yeah, I did too.'

'So how do you catch a touchy squid then?'

'You've got to go slow, real slow.'

'Why?'

'Because then it starts to trust you.'

'Can I have a go?'

'Sure.'

I handed her the line.

She held it for a while, moving it slightly, feeling the weight on it.

'It's like flying a kite,' she said.

'Haven't you ever been squidding before?'

'Never.'

Maybe living in the city wasn't all it was cracked up to be.

'You can pull it in if you like,' I said. 'But remember, slow and steady, no jerking.'

'Okay,' she said.

Neither of us said anything for a while.

Then Cathy said, 'You don't talk much, do you? I mean, when you're not talking about sheeps and squids?'

'I suppose not. Not compared to those Maccas, anyway.'

She smiled when I said this.

'They never shut up, those two. I tell you, I'm pretty sick of hearing about radical re-entries and gnarly left-handers.'

'What are youse doing?'

Pickles. He was whirling the jig around in a circle, like a cowboy with a lasso.

'Got a squid on,' said Cathy. 'A touchy one.'

'Blacky better take care of that,' said Pickles.

'Cathy's going okay,' I said.

Pickles gave me a dirty look. Girls and squid, according to him, didn't go together. When my sisters came down the jetty squidding, he gave them a really hard time.

She *was* going okay, too. Little coils of wet line were dropping neatly at her feet.

'I reckon this squid is really starting to trust me,' she said.

Pickles snorted.

'Must be almost here,' I said, looking over the side into the murky green water. Then I saw it, down deep, the dark shape of a squid.

'There it is,' I said.

'What do I do now? Pull it in?' said Cathy.

'You can't,' said Pickles.

'Why not?'

'Because that's a slock, it doesn't have any hooks,' I said.

'Then how do we catch it?'

'With the jig, that thing Pickles is holding. Just keep pulling it in.'

When the squid got near to the surface, it let go of the fish. Pickles threw the jig in. He jerked the line, making the jig dart around like a fish.

Suddenly the squid appeared from behind a pylon. It snatched at the jig with its tentacles. Pickles heaved at the line, and the squid was on, the hooks buried deep in its flesh.

'Got him!' he said, and he started pulling it in.

'Wow! Look at my squid,' said Cathy as it rose out of the water.

He'd almost got it level with the jetty when I

noticed the nasty look on his face. I'd seen that look before – Pickles was up to no good. Then I realised what it was – Cathy was standing next to him, her woolly white jumper was right in the firing line.

'Cathy! Stand back,' I said.

But she was looking at the squid, she didn't hear.

I stepped in front of her, just as Pickles flicked the squid over his shoulder. A jet of oily black ink flew through the air. And I copped it. Right in the face. The world turned inky black.

'Are you okay?' said Cathy. 'Here, take this.'

I wiped the ink out of my eyes.

'Yeah, I'm okay.'

'Sorry,' said Pickles, smirking. 'Accident.'

The squid was lying on the jetty, its tentacles squirming, its skin changing colour. It was making weird sucking noises.

'What's it doing?' said Cathy.

'Dying, I suppose,' I said.

'Not any more,' said Pickles and he threw his knife. It spun three times and the blade sliced into the squid's head. Right between the eyes. I have to admit, it was pretty impressive. The squid's tentacles stopped moving. It turned white.

'Oh, my poor squid,' said Cathy. 'And it trusted me.'

I could see a figure, all in white, walking up the jetty. It was Cathy's old man, the tennis player. I could see, when he got to us, that he wasn't happy, like he'd just lost three sets in a row.

'We've all been waiting for you,' he said. 'What've you been doing?'

'Catching a squid, Daddy.'

He looked down at the squid. He didn't seem too impressed.

'Well, come along then. Everybody's in the car waiting.'

'See you, Blacky,' said Cathy. 'Maybe up the jetty tomorrow.'

'See you,' I said.

After she was gone Pickles said, 'You've got the hots for her, haven't you?'

'Pig's bum I have,' I said, as I slipped the inky hanky into my pocket.

27

When I got home the three little ones were outside, playing hopscotch.

'You look sick again,' said Greggy.

He was standing on one leg, a stone in his hand.

'Do I?' I said.

'Same like before. Did you get bitten again?'

'Smitten, not bitten.'

'That's right, smitten. Did you get smitten again?'

'Yeah. S'pose I did.'

'By that same girl?'

'By that same girl.'

'Worser this time?'

'Worser.'

Much worser.

28

Yesterday's clouds had slinked off, ashamed of themselves. The sky looked even bluer than before, like it had been scoured clean. And the gang was in the usual place.

As I got nearer I could hear Cathy telling one of the Maccas, 'And this squid, you should have seen it squelching all over the place, it was amazing.'

Then she saw me.

'Here he is, the squid hunter.'

'Hi,' I said, a little embarrassed.

I went to put my towel next to Mark Arks.

'Why don't you put your towel down here next to me?' said Cathy.

'Excuse me?' I said.

For a second I thought she'd said, why don't you put your towel down here next to me?

'Put your towel down here,' she said, patting the space beside her.

Oh my God! She had.

So I put my towel down, but not too close, about an arm's length from her.

'I don't bite, you know,' she said.

I dragged the towel across a bit, then I took off my t-shirt and lay down.

'Cathy,' said the closest Macca, 'what does trans-mogrify mean?'

He had a surf magazine open in front of him.

'How do you spell it?' she said.

Macca spelled it out.

'I don't know,' she said. 'They probably made it up. You know what those surf mags are like.'

'It means when something changes into something else that's really bizarre,' I said.

'You sure about that?' said the Macca.

'Pretty sure,' I said.

I was dead sure. Increase Your Word Power. *Reader's Digest*.

'You know,' said Cathy, 'for somebody from the country you're pretty brainy.'

'Thanks,' I said.

'You should go to college. You could go to Kings with the skeg-head here.'

She elbowed Macca.

'Do you reckon they'd let me in?' I said.

'Sure,' she said.

'Would I have to sit an exam or something?'

'An exam?'

'Yeah, you know – a test. To see how brainy you are.'

'Of course not.'

'Then how do you get in?'

'Pay the fees.'

'You gotta pay to go to college?'

'Of course you've got to pay. I take back what I said about you being brainy.'

'It costs a packet to go to Kings,' said the Macca. 'Heaps more than any other school.'

'So if my olds paid the fees, I could go to Kings, too?' I said.

'Sure,' said Cathy.

I waited for the Macca to come up with a reason why I couldn't go to Kings. But he didn't.

'And if Pickles's old man paid the fees, he could go, too?'

Cathy looked across at Pickles. He was wearing the same clothes as yesterday. They were covered in squid ink. He was scratching away at his munga.

'I reckon they might draw the line there,' she said.

So going to Kings had nothing to do with brains, and everything to do with money, the folding stuff, as the old man called it. My day was getting better and better. It was about to get better still.

Cathy turned towards me.

'Can you do me a favour?' she said.

Could I do her a favour? Cathy, I wanted to say, all you have to do is ask. A belly flop from the lighthouse? Of course. Crawl naked on my belly to Kapoona and back? Straightaway. Eat a jar of Pickles's gents? With pleasure. For you, Cathy, I'd do anything.

Instead I said, 'Yeah, sure.'

'Put some oil on my back for me,' she said.

For a second I thought she'd said, put some oil on my back for me.

'Pardon?' I said.

'Put some oil on my back for me. The sun's getting hotter.'

'Um, yeah, sure, of course,' I said.

She rummaged in her bag, and then handed me the bottle. Tropical Island Deep Tanning Oil. Then she lay down, her elbows out, her chin resting on her hands.

I knelt down next to her and unscrewed the lid. My hands were shaking.

'Where do you want it?' I asked.

'All over,' she said. 'Slop it on.'

I squeezed the bottle. Oil squirted out. The smell was intense, exotic. A little pool of it lay in the small of her back.

'You have to rub it in,' she said.

I touched it with my fingertips. It was warm. Little jolts of electricity shot up my fingers. I started smoothing it across her back. I could feel the little corrugations of her vertebrae.

Her back was glistening.

'Is that okay?' I said, softly.

'That's great,' she said. 'Can you do my shoulders now?'

Her hair, in a plait, lay along her back. It reminded me somehow of a rope, one of those big ones they use to tie up ocean liners. I gently lifted it – I was surprised at how heavy it was, you don't think of hair as being heavy – and moved it out of the way.

Then I squeezed the bottle again. More oil squirted out.

If I die now, I said to myself, if a huge tidal wave, like in those Japanese horror movies, appears on the horizon, and carries me to watery oblivion, then I wouldn't care. I'd die happy, contented.

The sound of thongs flip-flopping. Somebody had arrived. I looked up. It was Deano.

'There's some Nungas heading this way,' he said. 'A big mob of 'em.'

Everybody looked up.

Usually the Nungas came into town, got their supplies and left again. But sometimes a mob would walk all the way from the Point. I'd heard them talking in the front bar about the good old days, about huge brawls down the jetty, Nungas against Goonyas. But I'd never been in one. I wouldn't want to, either. Those Nungas were tough, much tougher than us.

'Where are they?'

'They're coming down the main street.'

'How many?'

'Dunno. Fifteen, twenty, a lot.'

'What is it?' said Cathy, sitting up.

'Boongs,' said Pickles.

'What?' said Cathy.

'Abos,' said one of the Maccas. 'Coming up here. A tribe of 'em.'

'Are they allowed up here?' said Cathy

'Yeah, of course they are,' I said.

'They shouldn't be,' said Pickles. 'It's our jetty, not theirs.'

'Bloody oath,' said Deano.

I could see them now, at the start of the jetty. They were mucking around with the ropes that went out to the dinghies.

'If they touch our dinghy,' said Pickles, 'I'm gunna go get the old man.'

But they didn't. They kept going until they reached the steps. The camper kids, who were swimming there, moved out of the way. Then one of the Nungas, a girl, jumped in. She was wearing baggy shorts and a t-shirt. From the distance it looked like Clarence.

I could hear one of the others yelling, 'Hey Clar, what that water like? Cold, unna?'

It was Clarence. The others jumped in too.

'Don't they wear bathers?' said Cathy.

'Nuh, too shamed,' said Pickles.

Then they all got out again.

'Are they coming up here?' said Cathy.

She sounded scared.

'Maybe,' I said. But I was hoping they wouldn't.

They did though. Laughing and yelling, their

clothes dripping water. As they walked past, I pressed my face against the towel, hoping Clarence wouldn't recognise me. When they got to the end of the jetty they started climbing on the lighthouse.

'We should call the cops. They're not allowed up there,' said Mark Arks (who was always dropping bombs off the lighthouse).

Again, Clarence was the first to jump off. The others followed. Then they all clambered back up onto the jetty, and started walking back.

I put my head down again.

'Hey, Blacky, that's your girlfriend, isn't it?' said Pickles, loudly. 'What's-her-name?'

I don't know if Clarence heard. She didn't stop or say anything. She kept walking.

'That Abo wasn't really your girlfriend?' asked Cathy, when they'd gone.

'No way. It's Pickles' idea of a joke. Pathetic as usual.'

'But you know her?'

I hesitated.

'No, of course not. How would I know her?'

I screwed the lid back on the Tropical Island Deep Tanning Oil.

'Here you go,' I said, handing it back to Cathy.

'Thanks,' she said. 'You've got nice hands, you know. Gentle.'

'Thanks,' I said, but somehow the most perfect morning of my life wasn't so perfect any more.

29

'Wake up!'

I opened my eyes. It was early morning. Team-man standing at the side of my bunk.

'Piss off, will ya,' I said, pulling the sheet over my head.

'No, wake up. There's been a shooting!'

'Bullshit.'

'Fair dinkum. Down at the pub.'

'Pull the other one.'

'Would I make something like that up?'

I pulled the sheet down. Team-man had a point. He was incapable of making anything like that up. It had to be true.

The sun was just coming up as we got to the pub.

It was cordoned off. There were police cars everywhere, and one, two, three ambulances. Cops all over the place. There were other men, in plain clothes, coming in and out of the pub.

'Detectives,' said Team-man.

There was a huge crowd, pressing up against the tape. Locals and campers. Grown-ups wearing dressing-gowns, kids in pyjamas. I could see Shirl and Mick, Arks, Dazza and Pickles, Rocker, Slogs, the Maccas – everybody was there.

I could feel the excitement inside me swelling, getting bigger and bigger. At last something had happened in our hopeless little town. Not just a premiership. Something really important.

It'd be in the papers. Front page. Probably even on the telly.

All around me people were talking.

'Robbing the joint, they were.'

'Three got shot.'

'Killed two of 'em.'

'Who got shot?' I said.

'Dunno.'

'Nobody knows.'

'Boongs, that's all I know.'

'Serves 'em right, I reckon.'

'That's a bit tough, mate.'

'No, Big Mac done the right thing.'

'Look, they're bringing one out now.'

Two ambulance officers were carrying a stretcher through the front door of the pub. On it was a body, a lumpy shape covered in a white sheet.

I pushed through the crowd, right to the front. The tape was against my chest.

'Stand back, son,' said one of the cops. 'Stop pushing there.'

'Who's that on the stretcher?' I said. 'What's his name?'

'I don't know, son,' said the cop in that typical cop's voice. 'And even if I did I wouldn't be at liberty to tell you. The names will be released in due course.'

The front of the stretcher was resting on the back of the ambulance. The two officers were about to push it in when a gust of wind caught the corner of the sheet, lifting it up.

I could see a basketball boot. With a red star on the side. And red laces.

My guts froze. It was Dumby's shoe.

I stumbled back through the crowd.

'Steady there, Blacky,' somebody said.

'Why luv, you're as white as a sheet,' said Shirl.

I ran over to the anchor and sat down.

Dumby dead?

It couldn't be.

But that was his boot, nobody else had boots like that.

Maybe somebody borrowed them, or stole them. But I knew they hadn't.

Dumby Red was dead. Not bang bang you're dead, count to ten. Bang bang you're dead. That's it.

He was dead, and he'd been killed by Big Mac.

I could feel the bile rising in my throat. I leant over the anchor and let it all come streaming out.

30

In a town where nothing had happened in the last couple of hundred years, except a second in the Tidy Town Comp. (Section B) and a footy premiership, the pub shootings became the topic of every conversation. No matter where you were in the Port – up the jetty, down the beach, at the shops, in church – that's all people talked about. Nobody bothered with the weather any more. And everybody was an expert, everybody had their own version of what happened that night.

This is just one of them.

It's the Monday night of a hot, thirsty long weekend. Three days' takings are on the premises.

The only person in the pub is Big Mac. He's asleep, exhausted.

There's a noise outside, the crunch of gravel. Big Mac wakes up. He looks at the illuminated dial of his bedside clock – 2:35. Somebody's been down the jetty fishing, he thinks. They're walking home past the pub. He turns over, closes his eyes again.

The dog barks. Dumb mutt! Barks at its own shadow. Worst bloody guard dog I ever had.

The dog barks again. Louder this time. More insistently. Then there are footsteps on the gravel, people running. Followed by the sound of glass breaking, wood splintering. Somebody's breaking in.

Big Mac throws the covers off, swings his legs around, pulls his trousers on.

The door is flung open. One, two, three men barge into the bedroom. They have stockings over their heads. One of them is carrying a rifle.

'The safe. Come on,' he says.

'Steady on,' says Big Mac.

They push him out of the bedroom and towards the office. A gun is gnawing away at his ribs.

'Door's locked. I need the keys,' says Big Mac. 'They're over there.'

He points to the storeroom.

'Get 'em.'

He starts walking slowly. Nobody follows. The pressure at his ribs disappears. He opens the screen door. The keys are hanging on a nail. He slips them off with his right hand, his left hand gropes in the darkness. Until it finds what it was looking for – the barrel of a semi-automatic shotgun.

He steps deeper into the gloom of the storeroom.

'Where the fuck is he?' says one of the intruders.

Big Mac is trembling, his heart thumping. He flicks the safety and sticks the barrel through a hole in the mesh.

Maybe I should just warn them, he thinks.

But then he hears, 'Go get the fat prick.'

He squeezes the trigger. The gun bucks, noise fills the room. Somebody screams. Somebody else yells, 'A gun. He's got a fucking gun!'

Again he squeezes. More screams. And again. And again. Until the magazine is empty.

The air is full of thin, acrid smoke. He peeks through the screen. On the floor he sees three bodies. Two of them aren't moving, the third is moaning, kicking his leg, like a rabbit caught in a trap, smearing blood across the floor.

Big Mac turns around, picks up the phone, and dials. Zero. Zero. Zero.

'Dean, it's Mac, sorry to wake ya. You better come quick, there's been some trouble down here. Big trouble.'

A car starts up outside, and takes off with a squeal of rubber.

31

Once, ages ago, I was looking after Greggy.

'Can I do some colouring in?' he said.

'Yeah, sure,' I said. I opened his book. 'Do this page, this is a nice one.'

It was one of those typical beach scenes. You know — Mum, Dad and the kids down for a day at the seashore.

'Okay,' said Greggy.

He liked colouring in.

The cricket was on the telly. Australia was batting. It was pretty exciting. I didn't take much notice of what Greggy was doing. I could hear the scratch of the pencil on the paper.

'Finished,' he said. 'You wanna have a look?'

'Sure. Give it here.'

That kid. He'd only used one pencil – the grey. And he'd coloured the whole thing grey. Mum. Dad. Kids. Sandcastles. Sand. Seagulls. Sailing boats. The water and the sky. Even the sun. Grey.

That's exactly how everything looked after the shooting. That's how I felt, too. Inside and outside. Grey and heavy, like lead, like a sinker. If they dropped me off the jetty I'd plummet straight to the bottom, tiny air bubbles trailing behind.

32

'Aren't you going out today?' said Mum. She had a newspaper in her hand.

I was on the couch.

'I'll probably just hang around here. Maybe watch the cricket,' I said.

'I'm worried about you, Gary. You've been lying on that couch for days now. Are you sure you're feeling okay?'

'I'm fine, Mum.'

'You sure you don't want to go see Doc Matthews?'

I could imagine it.

'Yes, son,' says old Doc Matthews, with his baggy suit and tobacco-smelly breath, 'what's the matter with you today? That eardrum again is it?'

'That's my brother, doctor.'

'Yes, so it is. You're the boy with the groin, that's right. Still giving you some bother?'

'No, groin's fine, doctor. Actually it's a problem I have with the grey.'

'Yes, I see.'

'The whole world has turned sort of grey. Not only that, I feel grey too. Sad, I suppose.'

'Hmmm. Open your mouth and say aaaah.'

'Aaaah.'

'Bowel movements regular?'

'Pretty regular, doctor.'

He takes out his pad and starts scribbling.

'Let's start you off on a course of antibiotics. That should clear it up.'

No, I didn't want to see Doc Matthews.

'No, Mum, I'll be okay. Is that this week's *Gazette*?'

'Yes.'

'Can I have it?'

'Yes, but please don't leave it scattered all over the place. You know what your father's like.'

'Tension High Between Towns' said the headline. Publican Victor McRae had left the town. No charges were expected to be laid against him. Police suspected others were involved but so far had not taken anybody in for questioning. There had been a spate of robberies at hotels on the peninsula. Police suspected the same gang was involved in all of them.

Then, at the back I found it, the notice for Dumby's funeral service. It was going to be held at the Point, 10:30 Sunday. I tore the page out, folded it carefully into a square, and put it in my back pocket.

By this time Mum was out the back, an empty clothes basket on her hip. The wind was changing direction, swinging around to the south. It was getting stronger, too. Mum's dress was whipping around her legs, the clothes on the line were fluttering like flags.

'Mum, I wanna go to the funeral,' I said.

'What funeral's that?' she said, unpegging a shirt.

'Dumby's. It's on Sunday.'

'His poor mother,' said Mum.

'Can I go, then? I really want to.'

She said nothing, but continued unpegging clothes. By the time she'd come to the end of the row, the basket was half full.

'I understand why you want to go, dear. But I don't think you'd be welcome. It's for the people out there at the Point. It's their business, not ours.'

I started to walk away.

'We can send some flowers, if you like,' she said.

Arks was alone in his shop. The *Gazette* was spread out on the counter.

'Terrible business,' he said, shaking his head, clicking his tongue. 'Terrible business.'

Terrible for business, too, I thought. Ever since the shooting, the Nungas had stopped coming into town. They'd been going to Kapoona to buy their supplies even though it was twice as far.

'Did you see in the back? Dumby's funeral's on Sunday,' I said.

'That boy had so much talent,' said Arks. 'Talent to

burn. He could've gone anywhere. That mark he took.'

Arks raised his arms, spread his fingers wide, like he was taking the mark again.

'I've never seen anything like it. Never. He did go and spoil it all with that stupid pass. But still, it was one helluva grab.'

'Is the club doing anything?' I said.

'The club?' said Arks.

'Yeah, the footy club. Are they doing anything for Dumby's funeral? He was one of our players, wasn't he?'

'No, I don't think so, Blacky. Sport's one thing, this is another. It's better not to get the two mixed up.'

Then his tone changed.

'Looks like we'll be playing you up forward next season, after all,' he added.

I walked out, slamming the door as hard as I could. Except it didn't – it had one of those stupid door-closer things on it.

Didn't Arks realise there wouldn't be any team next year? Did he think the Nungas were still going to play for the Port after what happened?

Dazza and Pickles were sitting in the shed, right under 'BOONGS PISS OFF'. I could smell cigarette smoke.

'Dumby's funeral's on Sunday,' I said.

'And?' said Pickles.

'And I reckon we should do something.'

'Like what?' said Dazza.

'I dunno, just something.'

'The old man reckons he got what he deserved,' said

Pickles. 'Armed robbery, mate. It's serious shit.'

'Yeah,' said Dazza, 'play with fire and ya gunna get burnt.'

I walked away, shaking my head, not saying anything.

Darcy was in his usual possie.

'How's it going?' I said.

'Only got a couple,' he said. 'And I don't believe I'll be here much longer, not with that storm brewing up out there.'

He pointed towards the south where there was a huge bank of black clouds.

'What do ya reckon about what happened at the pub?' I said.

Darcy was probably the only person in town who wasn't a self-appointed expert. I hadn't heard him even mention the shooting.

He took a while before he answered.

'Not the first time you know, young'un.'

'What, that somebody got shot in the pub?'

'That there was killing in these parts.'

'But they didn't deserve to get killed, did they? Dumby was just a kid like me.'

'No, young'un, probably not. But there's always killing. Always has been. Always will be. It's human nature, there's no escaping it.'

He started reeling in his line.

'Reckon I'll be getting on home,' he said. 'Wanna walk with me?'

'No. I'll stay here for a while.'

'You be careful, young'un. That storm's in a big hurry. Mind you don't get caught in it, you'll catch your death.'

'Don't worry, Darce. I'm a big boy now. See ya later.'

I lowered myself over the side of the jetty, my feet searching for the familiar footholds. I sat on the cross-beam, exactly where Clarence had been that night. It was high tide; my dangling feet almost touched the crests of the waves. I hooked my arm around the pylon. It felt warm and smooth. My eyes followed it down as it entered the water. It became shaggy with weed, encrusted with barnacles and sponges. Little fish flitted around its edges.

It was quiet down there, just the sound of the waves as they rolled past and the slow creaking of the jetty.

Mum, Arks, Pickles, Dazza and Darcy – they all had different reasons, but they all said the same thing: don't go to Dumby's funeral.

I could smell the storm now. There was a rumble of thunder. Then the rain started, slanting into the sea, countless little pock-marks dancing over the surface.

When the squall had passed, and the rain stopped, I climbed back to the top. The air was fresh now. The smell of wet wood was rising from the soaked jetty.

As I started walking I realised I'd made a decision. I was going to the funeral. I looked towards the Point. I didn't care what anybody said. Tomorrow I was going to Dumby Red's funeral.

'Blacky!'

It was Cathy.

'You walked right past me. Like you were in a trance. Where've you been the last few days?'

'Doing stuff at home. Helping Mum.'

'You want to walk up to the end with me?'

'I can't. I've gotta go home. Get ready.'

'Get ready for what?'

'For tomorrow.'

'It's only a barbie,' she said.

I'd forgotten. Cathy had invited me to a barbie at her place. She was leaving on Monday. I was the only local she'd asked.

'You don't have to bring anything, silly,' she said, smiling.

She looked so beautiful. Her white teeth against her tanned face against the cloudy grey sky.

'I know,' I said. 'But there are some other things I've gotta do.'

'Okay,' she said. 'See you tomorrow then.'

'See you,' I said.

But I didn't.

33

Sharon was bouncing a tennis ball against the side of the house.

'Dad wants to see you,' she said as I passed

The three little ones were playing in a puddle.

'Have you seen Dad yet?' said the first one.

'He asked us where you were,' said the second.

'He looked pretty mad,' said the third.

I went inside.

Team-man was sprawled on the lounge, watching the cricket. Australia versus England.

'How's it going?' I said.

'Killing them. We're none for ninety-seven,' said Team-man. 'And the old man's been looking for you.'

'So I've heard. Do you know what for?'

'Dunno. Ask Mum. She's in the laundry.'

She was sorting the whites from the coloureds.

'Your father wants to see you,' she said.

'Do you know what for?'

'No, you'd better ask him.'

'Need a hand with that?' I said.

'I think you better see him first. He's in the shed.'

The old man's shed was behind the house. It was really a garage, with a roller door in the front. There was no room for a car inside though, not with all that stuff. Along one side hung the old man's tools. Shelves ran along the other. They were crammed with boxes of nails, jars full of screws, packets of washers, and a million other bits and pieces that didn't even have names. Right in the middle of the shed was a huge wooden workbench.

The old man kept the shed locked and the key was always with him. Us kids weren't allowed in there by ourselves. No way.

The door was up and the radio was on. An outboard motor was clamped onto the workbench. The old man was undoing something on it with a spanner. As usual he was wearing overalls and his shirt sleeves were rolled right up. He loved taking that outboard apart. He did it all the time. He'd strip it down, meticulously clean all the parts with kero, then put it all back together again.

'Australia are a hundred without loss and batting beautifully,' said the commentator on the radio.

The old man stopped to take a gulp of beer from a stubby.

I stepped inside.

'Hi,' I said.

'What have I told you about doing a job properly?' he said, glaring.

Here we go, I thought, the old if-a-job's-worth-doing-it's-worth-doing-properly lecture.

'If a job's worth doing it's worth doing properly,' I said.

'What's that?' he said, cupping his hand around his ear.

'If a job's worth doing it's worth doing properly,' I repeated, louder this time.

He'd made me write it out once. A thousand times. I cheated, of course. I just wrote 'if' all the way down the page, then 'a', then 'job' and so on, like that.

'That's right. If a job's worth doing then it's worth doing properly,' he said.

'He's snicked it! And he's out! Caught behind for forty-seven.'

'Damn!' said the old man.

He only listened to the cricket when we played the Poms. He hated the Poms. Mum's father was a Pom, and the old man was always giving her a hard time about it.

'Australia were going well too, weren't they?' I said.

But he wasn't about to get sidetracked.

'What happened to the lawn this week?'

The old man was the only one who called it a lawn. To us it was just the back yard, full of rocks and sporadic tufts of grass. Ages ago he'd planted some grass, and for a while there was a lawn. But then there was a drought, and water restrictions. His lawn died. But in his eyes it was still there, green and luscious. I hated mowing the back yard. Rocks flew up and took great chunks out of your shins.

'I forgot,' I said.

'Forgot, eh? Well listen to me. You're thirteen now and – '

'I'm fourteen,' I said, interrupting.

'Eh?'

'I'm fourteen.'

'That's what I said, isn't it? You're fourteen now, and it's about time you started pulling your own weight. When I was your age I was digging ditches for two bob an hour and coming home to a meal of bread and bloody dripping.'

The old bread and bloody dripping story. I'd asked Darcy about that, and he said, 'Goodness me, of course we never ate bread and dripping. Things were tough in them days, but not that tough.'

The old man put the stubby down, and picked up the spanner.

'Reggy can't make it tomorrow. He's back on the booze.'

The old man and Mick weren't partners any more. The old man had decided to go it alone. Fishing? Nothing to it, I tell ya. Money for old rope. But like I told you before, the old man didn't understand the sea. He had a good boat and he was strong but that wasn't enough. He didn't have the know-how. He caught bugger-all. Then he started taking Reggy Porter out.

Reggy Porter had the know-how all right. But Reggy Porter was a drunk, a hopeless one.

'You and your brother can give me a hand.'

'But you said you never wanted me on your boat again,' I said.

'Well, I've changed my mind. I'm giving you another chance.'

'But but but ... I can't come.'

'Why not?'

I couldn't tell him about Dumby's funeral.

'Because of ...'

The old man just stood there, looking at me, while I tried to come up with a plausible excuse. But then I realised I already had one.

'Because of Cathy's barbie. That's right, Cathy's having a barbie tomorrow.'

'Who?'

'Cathy. She's a camper. A friend of the Maccas.'

'Well you better tell this Cathy you can't come.'

'But ...'

'No buts about it. You're going fishing tomorrow.'

'Out!' said the commentator on the radio. 'Leg before for fifty-six.'

'Damn!' said the old man.

Right then, for the first time in my life, I found myself barracking for the Poms.

I started to walk away.

'We'll be leaving at seven. Be ready,' said the old man.

That was that. Now there was no way I could go to the funeral. If I didn't go out fishing with the old man, he'd kill me. I'm not joking, he'd spiflicate me.

Back inside, the Brady Bunchers were watching 'The Brady Bunch'. It was against my principles as a Gilligan's Islander, but what the heck, I sat down too. Greg (one of the kids) had a problem. He was telling Mike (the dad) about it.

'Gee, Greg,' said Mike, 'that's a tough one.'

But I knew Mike would still give Greg some good advice. Mike always gave good advice. So did Carol (the mum). Even Alice (the maid) gave good advice. That's why I hated 'The Brady Bunch' so much. It was so unlike real life. My life anyway. Grown-ups didn't solve problems, they made them.

'I know it is, Pop,' said Greg, 'but I was kind of hoping you could help me.'

Then there was an ad break. It gave Mike plenty of time to come up with just the right advice.

'All I can say,' he said, putting his arm around his son's shoulder, 'is to do what your heart tells you, Greg.'

'Do what my heart tells me, Pop?'

'That's right, Greg, do what your heart tells you.'

Greg looked a little perplexed. I couldn't blame him. What sort of advice was that?

'This program really sucks,' I said.

'Well you don't have to watch it,' said a Brady Buncher.

'Yeah, piss off,' said another.

I took the Brady Buncher's advice, and pissed right off, down to Bum Rock. I sat there for ages, watching the sun sink behind the island.

'Where you been?' asked Shaz when I got back.

'Bum Rock.'

'Where?'

'Black Rock.'

'Oh. What were you doing?'

'Not much. Just thinking about something.'

'About what?'

'About something Mike said on "The Brady Bunch".'

She looked at me in disbelief.

'But we despise "The Brady Bunch",' she said.

'I know we do, but still, I can't get it out of my head.'

'So what did Mike say?'

'Do what your heart tells you to do.'

Shaz look worried. I can't blame her. If I defected to the Brady Bunchers, took my fourteen votes, then Gilligan, the Professor and Mary-Anne would never appear on our telly again.

'Well, my heart's telling me it needs an ice-cream,' said Shaz. 'You wanna come down the shop and get one?'

'No, thanks,' I said.

Shaz looked even more worried.

'My shout,' she said.

'Thanks, but I've got something to do,' I said, and I walked away.

'A double-header,' she yelled after me.

It was quiet in the bedroom, there was nobody there. I lay on my bunk and stared at the scar. And I listened. I listened very carefully.

And when I finished listening I got my footy bag out of the cupboard. There was a crusty old sock inside. I tossed it under Team-man's bunk. Then I got my best pants out, the ones I used to wear to church, before I decided I was an agnostic. I found my white school shirt, and good school shoes. I put them all inside the bag. There was only one thing missing – a tie. I'd never been to a funeral before but I knew you were supposed to wear one.

I couldn't find my school tie anywhere. I didn't want to ask Mum, she'd get suspicious. But I remembered having once seen the old man with a tie on. I think it was to go to Rocker's wedding.

The old man was still in the shed. The outboard was almost back together again. Mum was sitting at the kitchen table, slouched forward, her head resting on her arm.

'Mum,' I said.

She didn't answer. She was sleeping.

I opened their bedroom door and slid in through the gap. I closed the door softly behind me. Then I opened the wardrobe. Considering he only ever wore overalls, the old man had a lot of clothes. But the tie wasn't hard to find. Even in the gloom it stood out. For a start it was purple. Bright purple. And it was wide, the widest tie I'd ever seen. I shoved it in my pocket and sneaked back out of the room.

I was ready.

More or less.

34

I woke early. There was still night in the room, lingering in the corners. The siblings were all asleep. I climbed down from my bunk. I'd slept with my clothes on, so all I had to do was grab my footy bag and climb out through the window. The sun was just coming up over the chook house. I walked carefully down the drive, past the window of my parents' bedroom. The gravel was sharp, but my feet were pretty tough. Then when I got to the road I started walking quickly, towards the Point, until the road narrowed, the bitumen became dirt, and the house was well out of sight. Then I got my breakfast out – a squishy banana and two Weetbix – and sat by the side of the road to eat it.

In front of me the sea was calm, moving slowly in and out, like it was breathing, sleeping against the rocky foreshore. I was feeling happy. The happiest I'd felt in a long time. Colour was seeping back into my world. It wasn't so grey any more. And somehow it didn't seem right. I was going to my mate Dumby's funeral after all. And when I got home my old man was going to spiflicate me. Still, you can't argue with how you feel, and I was feeling happy.

I tossed the peel onto the rocks and started walking, following the coast. After maybe an hour and a half I'd reached the sandhills. Here the road skirted around to the right.

I looked at my watch – there was plenty of time. I was already about halfway to the Point. I didn't want to get to the funeral early. Maybe somebody would tell me to go away.

'Hey, you whitefella. Piss off. This here's blackfellas' business, unna.'

There were huge piles of seaweed on the shore. I'm not sure why it collected there, something to do with the winds and the tides I suppose. I lay down. The seaweed felt springy, like a mattress. It was dry, but it still had a rich rotting smell. Close to shore a couple of shags were swimming about, their s-bend necks sticking out of the water. There were just a few streaky white clouds high in the sky; it was going to be a scorcher. Maybe people in the Port would even start talking about the weather again.

I started thinking about Dumby.

Deadly, unna? He was always saying that. All the Nungas did, but Dumby more than any of them.

'Good pie, Dumby?'

'Deadly, unna?'

'Did ya see Carlton on the replay?'

'Deadly, unna?'

And now Dumby was dead. Unna?

Claire told me that at Sunday School one of the kids had asked Mrs Ashburner if the boys who broke into the pub would go to heaven. She didn't like the question, Claire said. You could tell. But finally she said, 'It's for the good Lord to decide.'

Nice side-step, Mrs Ashburner.

And what would the good Lord decide? I wondered. What had Dumby done? He'd broken into the pub. Maybe he did have a gun like the cops said. He wasn't going to shoot anybody though. Not Dumby.

I had another question for Mrs Ashburner. What about Victor McRae? Would he go to heaven? He'd killed two people, after all. What about 'thou shalt not kill' and all that stuff?

But I knew what she'd say. The good Lord would have to decide on that one, too.

The sun was high overhead now. It was time to get changed. The pants and shirt were fine, not too creased at all. The shoes were a bit scruffy though. I gave them a bit of the old spit and polish. Then the tie – I hung it loosely around my neck. One of the shags drifted in for a closer look.

'Whatta ya reckon, shag?' I said.

It shook its sorry head.

Maybe the shag was right. Against the white of the

shirt, the tie looked even more purple. And wide. Geez it was wide – it looked like a bib. But then again, it was a funeral. And blokes wear ties to funerals. It's the done thing.

'Okay, shag, let's toss. Heads I wear the tie. Tails I don't.'

I tossed the coin. It spun through the air. And came down – heads.

'Best out of three,' I said.

I tossed again. Heads again. I had no choice. As I knotted the tie the shag swam off in disgust. Then I put my old clothes inside the footy bag and stuck it under a rock. I walked back up to the sandhills.

I'd never liked it there. The way the sand was always moving, shifting about, like it couldn't make up its mind. Not only that, it was infested with snakes. Crawling with them. I'd never actually seen one, but I knew they were there, staring at me as I hurried along the track. Their little black tongues flicking. It was a relief to get to the other side.

This was where Dazza and I had got to that day. Before we got scared shitless. There was a barbed-wire fence, with a sign on it. THE POINT ABORIGINAL RESERVE – NO ENTRY WITHOUT PRIOR PERMISSION it said. It was riddled with bullet holes.

I climbed through the bottom strands, making sure the tie didn't get caught. I'd let Cathy down, the old man was going to spiflicate me, and now I was breaking the law. I knew it – I should never have listened to Mike Brady.

The land here was dry and dead flat, no trees, just saltbushes and rocky outcrops. I could see the Point clearly now, in the distance, the houses glinting in the sun. The town itself wasn't actually on the point, it was inland a bit. It seemed a really dud place to stick a town, away from the sea, in the middle of nowhere like that.

The track joined up with the main road and continued into town. I didn't take it though. There were a few cars heading along the road, plumes of dust trailing behind them, and I didn't want to be seen until the very last minute. Instead I cut across the bush.

There was lots of rubbish around — broken bottles, an old mattress, plastic bags snagged on the bushes. And up ahead was the burnt-out shell of a car. It was on its back, like a dead cockroach. In the front bar they said the Nungas didn't put oil or water in their cars. When the warning lights on the dash started flashing, they just kept on driving, until the engine blew up. Then they'd set fire to it. The government always bought them another one, they said in the front bar. No worries.

This car hadn't been there long. There were scorch marks on the ground. And it had that smell, like when you throw something plastic in the incinerator. I wasn't great with cars, Dazza was the expert, but it looked a bit like a Valiant. Maybe it was the car the cops were looking for. But I wouldn't tell them about it. No way.

I reached the edge of town. There were a few

scraggy chooks scratching around, but I couldn't see any people. I kept walking.

The Point was not a big chance in the Tidy Towns competition, I can assure you of that. Not even in Section B. The streets weren't sealed and there were hardly any trees. Most of the houses were fibro, but there were a few brick ones as well.

I kept thinking. But that's not right, something's wrong.

Then I realised what it was. The houses all had doors and windows. And according to the front bar the first thing Nungas do when they move into a new house is rip the doors off their hinges and smash all the windows.

So that was the image I had in my head. No doors. No windows. Well, not any more.

Up ahead I saw a couple of boys kicking a plastic footy around. They were wearing shorts, but no shoes or shirts.

'Gidday,' I said.

They looked up, astonished, and took off. I picked up the footy. They stopped at the end of the street and turned around. I kicked the footy towards them (not a bad dob either). They took off again.

Maybe they thought I was some sort of white ghost. Maybe it was the tie.

I turned into another street. There were more kids, maybe ten or more, including the footballers, spread across the road. A couple were on bikes. They were all looking at me. Intently.

I took a step towards them. They scuttled back like crabs, laughing.

'Can you tell me where the funeral is?' I said, loudly.

They started talking amongst themselves. I could hear Dumby's name mentioned.

'It's that way, unna,' said a girl in a red t-shirt that came to her knees, pointing.

'Is it a long way?' I said.

'Yeah, long way,' she said.

I set off. The kids followed, keeping their distance.

I passed the primary school. There was a huge mural painted on the side of the wall. Kangaroos and boomerangs and stuff like that. Next door to the school was a large stone building. One of the walls was crumbling and half the roof was caved in, but it looked familiar somehow. Of course! It was our Institute. Exactly the same building, even the stone was the same colour. The two buildings must've been built around the same time. It made me realise – I knew nothing about the history of the Point. The Port's history, all that stuff about the windjammers, had been rammed down our throats. But they told us nothing about the Point.

Then I came to a t-junction. I hadn't seen a cemetery yet, and I was on the other side of town. I turned around. The girl in the red t-shirt pointed to the left, towards the coast. Obviously the cemetery was out of town. If it was a long way I'd miss the funeral. I started walking quickly. The kids didn't follow.

What a prize dickhead I was. I'd come all that way, and I was going to miss the funeral. I was going to get spiflicated, and all for nothing. And it was getting hot. I wiped my forehead with the tie. My shoes were hurting. I'd probably grown two sizes since the end of school.

Then I heard the sound of a car coming from behind. I thought about sticking my thumb out. Hitch-hiking to a funeral is probably not the done thing, I told myself. I moved to the side of the road. A Torana whizzed past, sending up a spurt of gravel. I could see a couple of black faces looking at me through the rear window. Then the brake lights came on, the wheels locked up and the car slid to a stop. It backed up quickly, the engine whirring, until it was level with me. The front window wound down.

'Blacky, what the hell ya doing out here?'

It was Clarence. The first time I'd seen her since that day up the jetty. She looked different. Her face was thinner. She looked tired.

'I was going to Dumby's funeral,' I said.

'That's a deadly tie you got there, Blacky,' she said.

She smiled, and I felt better. Then she turned around to say something to the other people in the car. I couldn't hear what they were talking about, but it sounded like an argument.

Eventually she opened the door.

'You better hop in then, brudda,' she said. 'Travel with us, Nunga-style.'

I squeezed in. The car was packed. Even more packed than our car on a Sunday drive. Everybody was young. And they were all dressed up. I noticed, with relief, that the boys were wearing ties. Perhaps not as vibrant as mine, but still ties.

'Hi,' I said.

There were a couple of grumbled replies, but nobody seemed that excited to see me.

'You know Lovely?' said Clarence, inclining her head towards the driver.

I didn't actually, but I knew his reputation. He'd played footy for the Port a few years ago. He was good too, as good as Dumby. Then he disappeared. 'Gone walkabout,' said Arks. Somebody, I think it was Pickles, said he'd got into strife, ended up in some sort of reform school.

'Gidday,' I said.

Lovely didn't say anything. He slammed the gears into first and dropped the clutch. We sped down the road.

My left hand gripped the door handle, the knuckles turning white.

Christ, I thought, why doesn't somebody tell him to slow down a bit?

Lovely turned to look at me.

'Whatta reckon, brudda?' he said, not smiling, his face hard.

'About what?' I said.

'About the fuckin' price of tommy ruffs?' he said 'Whatta ya think?'

I was scared. I could feel the anger in his voice, the car was sliding from one side of the road to the other.

'Leave 'im alone,' said Clarence. 'He's okay, he's

225

paying his respects that's all. Leave 'im alone.'

'Yeah, sure,' said Lovely.

'There it is,' said somebody from the back.

Up ahead I could see a group of cars. Lovely took his foot off the accelerator. I relaxed my grip on the handle.

We were almost at the end of the point. It was sandy out here, not rocky. The skeleton of a boat lay on the beach, half buried.

'It's over here,' said Clarence, as we got out of the car.

The cemetery was surrounded by an old iron fence, with a gate at one end. The paths inside were covered with shell grit, like we used to give to our chooks to make their eggshells strong. I could see a pile of sand on the other side. Dumby's grave, I thought. Imagine being lowered into that, deep into the ground, then covered in six foot of sand.

I followed Clarence to where a crowd of people were standing beneath a gum tree. Some of them were talking, softly, almost whispering. A gentle breeze was rustling the leaves in the tree. And in the distance was the sound of seagulls squawking. I could see Tommy and Sid and a few other people I knew from the footy, but I was the only Goonya there. Nobody said anything to me. I was starting to feel conspicuous, self-conscious. Maybe Mum was right after all, it was their business, Nungas' business. Nothing to do with me.

Then I noticed the coffin, resting on a trestle table. It was open, people filing past. I hadn't expected that.

'Come on,' said Clarence.

We joined the queue. I wasn't going to look, though. No way. I'd never seen a dead person before, let alone a dead friend.

But when it was my turn, I opened my eyes. I couldn't help myself. The first thing I noticed was the inside of the coffin. It was purple, like my tie. That made me feel better, somehow. Then I looked at Dumby. He was wearing a suit, even a tie, and black shoes, not his basketball boots. His hair was wrong. They'd combed it all wrong. Dumby never combed his hair like that. Typical, I thought, just because you're dead they think they can do what they like.

I ran the back of my finger along the side of the coffin. It felt smooth, cool.

Then something weird happened. The sounds in the background – the seagulls, the rustle of the leaves, the other people's voices – disappeared; they dissolved into silence. And I seemed to get swallowed up by this feeling, I don't know how to describe it – peace, I suppose. I stopped being angry because of Dumby's hair, I stopped feeling conspicuous because I was the only Goonya there. Instead this feeling of peace surrounded me.

Then I could hear somebody behind me gently clearing their throat. I looked up – everybody was staring at me, waiting. I moved on.

After that they buried Dumby, but I didn't watch. I didn't like the idea, it gave me the creeps. Besides, it was too hot, the glare from the white shell grit was burning my eyes and I'd forgotten to bring any water. I was starting to feel a bit woozy. I sat on the beach next to the wrecked boat.

The bay here was shallow. The tide was rushing out, rivulets of water were winding through the sand. Further out I could see sandbars sticking out like ribs. Egrets were pecking about on them. A couple of pelicans were drifting close to shore.

In the distance I could see the jetty – a blurry line floating above the water. Maybe Pickles and Dazza were sitting at the anchor right now, looking towards the Point, at exactly where I was sitting, telling each other stories they'd heard in the front bar. Wild Nungas with spears, boomerangs that come from nowhere and knock you senseless. What would they say if they knew I was there, looking right back at them? Not much probably. What had Dazza said? Play with fire and ya gunna get burnt. Maybe, Dazza, but not burnt to death.

I picked up a stone and flicked it. It skipped across the surface – one, two, three, four times.

'Hopeless.'

I looked behind, it was Clarence. She'd been crying, her cheeks were wet. She picked up a stone, brought her arm back and threw it with a snap of her wrist. The stone flew low and flat. When it hit the water it just kept going. One, two, three, four, five, six, seven, eight, nine skips.

'Far out!' I said.

'Average,' said Clarence.

'Hey, thanks for coming and all, brudda,' she said.

'Are you sure?'

'Course I'm sure. I said it, didn't I?'

'Don't think Lovely was too happy.'

'Lovely's crazy.'

She paused for a while. 'He was there, you know.'

I didn't say anything but I wasn't surprised.

'It was all Lovely's idea, and Dumby went cos Lovely's his hero.'

She picked up another stone, bouncing it up and down in the palm of her hand.

'Then Lovely leaves Dumby to die like a dog on the pub floor. Fuck Lovely. I wish he got killed, not Dumby.'

She was crying again. I didn't know what to do. What do you say to somebody whose brother has been shot dead? There, there, it'll be better in the morning. Clarence threw the stone. It flew through the air, hit the water, and sank.

'Anyway, how ya getting home?' she said.

'I'll walk. It's not far.'

'Not far my arse. Come on.'

There were only a couple of cars left. A group of older people were talking amongst themselves, under the gum tree.

'Mum,' said Clarence. 'Can Blacky come with us?'

Clarence's mother was short and solid. She had a big face, round like a dinner plate, and a broad nose. Her grey hair was cut short. She was wearing a black dress.

'Sure, he can come, if he don't mind travelling Nunga-style.'

The same joke as Clarence had made – if you don't mind travelling Nunga-style.

'When we going?'

'Dreckly. Soon as your daddy gets here,' she said.

I could see Tommy Red in the cemetery, next to Dumby's grave, his head bowed. Then he walked towards us. Slowly, like his legs were full of lead.

'Gidday, young Blacky,' he said when he saw me.

But it was hard to believe this was the same Tommy Red. Sometimes when we went catching crays, you'd see one but it'd be nothing but a shell. That's what Tommy reminded me of. Like his insides had gone, all those chug-a-lugs had disappeared.

I got in the front of the car, next to Clarence. Tommy Red drove slowly. Nobody said anything. Clarence turned the radio on and started pushing some buttons. She found a station. The beat of the song was the same as the clatter of the car across the corrugations on the road. Little specks of dust were dancing in the air.

'For Chrissakes turn that off!' said Tommy, his voice harsh and strained. 'This is a day of mourning, not a bloody rock concert.'

Clarence quickly pushed the off button.

'Mum,' said Clarence, as we entered the town, 'Blacky, he walk all the way here. Maybe somebody can drive him back to the Port.'

'Dreckly. First he can 'ave a cuppa tea and a scone back 'ome.'

230

We parked in front of a brick house. Along the front there was a row of geraniums, planted in powdered-milk tins.

The back yard was crowded. All the men. Most had taken their jackets off and loosened their ties. I could see Lovely, talking to Sid. It looked like they were arguing.

'Is Lovely really your cousin?' I asked Clarence as I followed her inside.

'You know we all cousins out the Point,' she said.

'But is he really your cousin? Is Sid Lovely's old man?'

'That's right.'

'And Sid is Tommy's brother?'

'That's right, too.'

'Then Lovely's your first cousin?'

Clarence smiled. The kitchen was crowded. I could smell scones baking. Tea was being made.

''Scuse me,' said Clarence's mum as she pushed past me with a huge teapot.

I was in the way, so I moved into the lounge room. There was an old lady there, sitting in a chair, wrapped in one of those multi-coloured rugs that near-sighted grannies crochet. Her head was tilted to one side and her eyes were closed.

I sat on the sofa. My bum sank right down, almost to the floor. The springs were busted – just like our sofa at home. Probably for the same reason too. Kids jumping up and down on it, pretending it was a trampoline.

I looked around the room. On top of the telly there was a photo of Dumby in his school uniform. Smiling his killer smile.

Clarence came into the room.

'Been looking for you. What ya doing hidin' in here? You wanna cuppa?' she said.

'Sure,' I said.

'Come into the kitchen, then. I'm not waiting on you.'

Clarence's mum was sitting at the kitchen table. She kicked her shoes off.

'That feels good,' she said. 'Get the weight offa me ankles.'

Then she pulled a seat out.

'Sit down,' she said.

'Thanks,' I said.

Clarence put a cup of tea in front of me.

I took a mouthful. It was the sweetest tea I'd ever tasted. My guess was at least five teaspoons of sugar.

'You one of them Blacks, are ya?' said Clarence's mum.

'Yeah. I'm the second eldest.'

'How many of youse, then?'

'Eight.'

'Christ Almighty, your poor mother.'

A plate of chunky, golden scones, appeared on the table. Clarence's mum pushed them towards me.

'Have one,' she said. 'Before they get cold.'

She looked over her shoulder.

'Clar, bring some jam an' butta for Blacky.'

Then she got up.

I sat there at the kitchen table for ages, the women bustling around me, and ate scones. One after another. Five all together. They were good those scones, as good as Mum's.

Then Clarence said, 'Blacky, Uncle Sid says he'll give you a lift. He's leaving now. Gotta see the cops 'bout something.'

The men were still all outside, except for Lovely – I couldn't see him. Tommy Red was sitting down, on an old car seat, his head in his hands.

'You ready?' said Sid.

'Sure,' I said.

I looked at Clarence.

'Nukkin ya,' I said.

'Yeah,' said Clarence. 'Nukkin ya. Maybe up the jetty, unna?'

So she had seen me that day. Or had she? I couldn't tell.

'Maybe up the jetty,' I said, and then I walked away.

Sid said nothing as he drove. He still had his suit on, but he'd taken his tie off and the top button of his shirt was undone. He had one hand on the wheel, the other elbow was leaning on the window. The cassette player was turned up loud. Slim Dusty.

'Could you stop at the sandhills?' I said. 'I left my bag there.'

He didn't really reply, but he stopped, and waited while I retrieved my bag. Then he drove on to the Port. We pulled up outside my house.

I noticed, with relief, that the old man's car wasn't there. The spiflicating would have to wait.

'Thanks for the ride. Thanks a lot,' I said, opening the door.

Sid put his hand lightly on my wrist.

'We 'preciate ya coming,' he said. 'All of us. Us mob ain't big speech makers and that but let me tell ya, we all 'preciated it.'

I shut the door, and he drove off.

'Where have you been?' said Mum as I walked through the door. 'I've been worried sick about you. And what are you doing with your good pants on? And your good shirt? And that's your father's tie you're wearing. And what's that all over it? It looks like jam.'

How could I get out of this one? What story could I come up with? My brain went into overdrive. But all it came up with was – Mum, I've been to Dumby's funeral. But I couldn't tell Mum that. It was the truth and the truth was the absolute last resort, only to be used when everything else had failed.

'Mum, I've been to Dumby's funeral,' I said.

'You've been where?'

'To Dumby's funeral.'

She looked at me for a while. She wasn't used to it either, the truth straight out like that.

'In that tie?' she said.

'It was the only one I could find.'

'Covered in jam?'

'That happened later.'

'Well, I hope nobody took exception,' she said.

234

There was a flicker of a smile on her lips.

'No, Mum, they didn't. Not at all.'

'That's good, now give me the tie and we'll put it back where it belongs.'

'Where's Dad?' I said, undoing the knot.

'Still not back,' she said. 'You better have something to eat and get to bed.'

It seemed like pretty good advice.

35

I woke up. It was dark.

Team-man was getting undressed, his back to me.

'Where you been all this time?' I said.

'Nowhere,' he said.

He turned around. His eyes were red, he'd been crying. There was blood smeared across his top lip.

'Christ, what happened to you?' I said.

'Nothing.'

Then he started crying and the words tumbled from his mouth.

'He wouldn't stop. He was looking for that ledge. You know the one where we caught all those snapper the day of the storm? "It's around here somewhere," he kept on saying. He didn't take his eyes off that stupid echo sounder. And he'd find a ledge and I'd throw my line in but there wasn't anything there. "That's not the right one," he'd say. "It's around here somewhere." And he was drinking all the time. Then it started to get dark. "Shouldn't we go home now?" I said. And he goes, "We're not going anywhere until we fill that fucking well." In the end he was so pissed he couldn't steer the boat. He just flaked out in the wheelhouse. So I took over. It was okay in the beginning, I just headed east but then I could see all these lighthouses blinking and I didn't know which one was the Port. Then he woke up. "Why aren't we still fishing?" he said and he chucked me out of the wheelhouse. That's how I got this.'

Team-man pointed to his lip.

'Then he turned the boat around. He was gunna go back out there "But we'll run out of fuel," I said. "Bullshit," he goes. But after a while he looked at the gauge and he turned around again. Then he started ranting about you. Like it was your fault. How he'd given you a chance to go fishing and prove you weren't a gutless wonder. He was just going on and on.'

There were tears running down Team-man's cheeks.

'I'm never going fishing with him again. Never, as long as I live.'

I'd never heard him talk like this about the old man.

'Where is he now?' I asked.

There was a crash from the kitchen. Then the old man's voice, loud and slurred.

'I'd keep out of his way if I were you,' said Team-man.

'Don't worry, I intend to,' I said.

There was another crash from the kitchen.

'What's he doing?' I said, but Team-man didn't answer, he'd fallen asleep.

I pulled the sheet over my head.

Another crash. More ranting.

Christ! Maybe he's coming to get me.

But then there was silence. He'd stopped ranting.

And it wasn't long before I too was in the land of nod.

36

It was late when I woke. Team-man was asleep, curled up like a baby, the blood still on his face. Greggy was playing with a truck, brrmm brrmm brrmming it along the floor, negotiating the various obstacles. The other siblings had gone.

I slid off the bunk.

'Where's the old man?' I asked Greggy.

'He went out,' he said.

'Are you sure?'

'Yeah, I'm sure.'

I looked out through the window. The car was gone.

'Anyway, where'd you go yesterday?' said Greggy. 'Mum was really worried. She almost called the police.'

'To a funeral.'

'A dead person's funeral?'

'Yeah, a dead person's funeral.'

'What was the dead person's name?'

'Dumby Red.'

'Who got shot down the pub.'

'That's right, him.'

'Did they bury him in a grave?'

'Yes, they buried him in a grave.'

'Was it scary?'

'Geez, I dunno. Stop asking so many questions, will you?'

'No need to get mad.'

'I'm not getting mad.'

'Yes, you are.'

'No, I'm not.'

But I probably was. What I needed was a shower. The hot water had run out but I didn't mind. The cold water on my skin felt great.

When I came back Greggy was still brrmming his truck

'Is that why Dad's mad at you?' he said.

'Who says he's mad at me?'

'He did this morning.'

'What did he say?'

'He said you were a heap of lard. And a bludger. Then he banged the table. Real hard.'

Team-man opened his eyes.

'He's mad at you, too,' said Greggy, pointing at him with his truck. 'Both of you.'

'Who cares,' I said. 'He's a psychopath.'

'What's that?' said Greggy.

'A mad man. A crazy. A loony,' said Team-man.

'No he's not!' said Greggy. 'You two are the psychopavs.'

And he brrmmed his truck right out of the room.

Poor Greggy. I was the same at his age. Hey, everybody! My dad's the best. My dad's the biggest. My dad's the strongest. The best of them all. I used to believe it, too. I really did. But then again I also believed that every year a fat man in a red suit used to squeeze down the chimney with a sackful of toys (and we didn't even have a chimney).

The sound of the radio floated down the corridor.

'This is the Rusty Nails morning program.'

All the deejays on our local station were called Rusty – Rusty Nails, Rusty Gates. I reckon that's how they got the job.

'Name, please.'

'Rusty Hinge.'

'Great, the job's yours.'

Rusty continued.

'And the weather for today. A strong to very strong wind warning for all coastal regions. An estimated top of forty-two degrees.'

Time for breakfast. Mum was sitting on a stool, at the bench. The sink was full of dishes. In front of her was a mug of coffee. Next to it an abalone shell (everybody in the Port used abalone shells for ashtrays), with a ciggie resting on it, a squiggle of smoke floating upwards.

'Morning,' I said.

'Morning, dear,' she said.

She sounded tired. She looked tired, too. There were smudges under her eyes. Her teeth weren't in. Her face looked drawn.

I put two pieces of bread in the toaster.

'What are your plans for today?' she said.

'Dunno. Probably just hang around the jetty.'

'Well, don't bother your father too much.'

Don't worry, Mum, I have no intention of bothering my father. In fact I intend to keep right out of his way. Which wasn't that difficult in a big family like ours. Maybe he'd come after me, but I doubted it somehow. It wasn't his way. He'd just keep it all inside. Like bottles of home brew that haven't been made properly. All that stuff inside fermenting away, until eventually it's too much and the bottle explodes. Shards of glass flying everywhere. That's what the old man was like.

'Okay, Mum.'

'And I might have to take the bus to Adelaide today. You grandfather's not feeling too well.'

Mum's father had been sick for ages, ever since I could remember.

'Okay, Mum.'

The toast popped up. The marg was already out. And as usual, it was disgusting. There were smears of Vegemite all over it, blobs of jam. It looked like some sort of weird abstract painting. Thanks, siblings. I really hated my family sometimes.

I dug deep with the knife, got some good marge

out, and spread it thickly on the toast. I was just deciding on Vegemite or jam when a car pulled into the drive. There was a flash of white across the window. A car door slammed. Jesus Christ, it was him! Maybe he was coming after me. I grabbed my toast.

'See ya, Mum. Gotta go.'

I bolted down the passage, into the bedroom. Teamman was getting dressed.

'What's wrong with you?' he said.

'Nothing,' I said. 'Here, you can have these.'

I dropped the toast on his bed, then I dived through the window. I could hear the old man's voice. He was yelling again. I started running, my thongs flapping, down the drive, across the road. Then I scrambled down the cliff and onto the rocks. Where could I go? Where could I spend the day? Bum Rock? No, the old man could see me through his binoculars. Under the jetty? No, he'd probably come looking for me there. Then I had a brainwave – Pickles's place. The old man didn't go there any more, not since him and Mick had stopped fishing. It was the perfect place.

Ramshackle, I reckon that's about the right word to describe the Pickles's place of abode. It looked like a grown-up's version of those houses Greggy made with playing cards. A few fibro sheets leaning up against each other, and some corrugated iron thrown on the top for a roof. But what was really amazing was the amount of junk that lay around the place – piles of nets, rusty chains, anchors, outboard motors that didn't work, an old dinghy, cray pots, fish traps, buoys, broken crates, tangled ropes, an old freezer, and a ute up on blocks that was full of feral chooks.

I knocked on the back door.

Nobody answered. So I walked around the side. Pickles' bedroom window was open. I could see him spreadeagled on his bed, still wearing his footy shorts, asleep.

'Pickles, rise and shine.'

He looked up, his eyes half open.

'Rack off,' he said.

I climbed in through the window.

Christ, what a pong, like your footy bag if you leave a wet towel in there all week. I sat on the foot of the bed and started bouncing it up and down.

'Wakey, wakey,' I said. 'Wakey, wakey.'

'Stop that!' said Pickles, sitting up. He had a good scratch at his munga. 'What time is it, anyway?'

'Round nine I think.'

'Why you talking like that?' he said.

I was trying not to breathe through my nose.

'Got a bit of a cold.'

There was a stack of jars next to the bed. I picked one up and gave it a shake. It was full of flies. They were all dead, except for Louis, the sole survivor, buzzing around the top.

'Gents not selling so well any more?' I said.

Pickles gave me a dirty look. I'm sure he thought I had something to do with his failure as a maggot entrepreneur, just because I was mates with Darcy. It had nothing to do with me, though. Blame the fish, Pickles.

Blame the tommies, flathead and gars. They're the ones who decided that your maggots weren't so yummy.

'Where were you yesterday, anyway?' said Pickles.

'Around,' I said.

'Around where?'

'Just around.'

'That bushpig, Cathy, was looking for ya. She gave me this.'

He handed me a tight square of paper.

I put in my pocket.

'Ain't ya gunna read it?' he said.

'Later.'

'It says you're dropped.'

Great. I'd been dropped, by a girl I wasn't even going with. My life was a joke.

'Doesn't worry me,' I said.

Pickles snickered.

'What are you doing today?' I said.

'Gotta meet Mad Dog. You wanna come?'

He was talking about our Mad Dog, not the Mad Dog from Tangaratta. Actually our Mad Dog was even madder then the Tangaratta Mad Dog. He had a steel plate in his head.

'Nuh. Why don't we just hang around here?'

'Hang around here! You gotta be joking.'

I had a look around. The room looked like Darwin after Cyclone Tracy. I can see why he thought I was joking.

'Is it okay if I do then, stay in your room?'

'Who you hiding from?' said Pickles.

My immediate thought was to bullshit, tell Pickles a lie. But then I thought, Bugger it, Pickles really is one of my best friends. I should tell him the truth. Maybe he could help me. Give me some support.

'The old man. He's after me.'

'You're joking! I wouldn't want your old man after me. No way. Remember that time he bashed that bloke up outside the pub? It was fuckin' awesome. There was blood running down the gutter. Remember that? I thought he was gunna kill him.'

'Thanks, Pickles. Thanks a lot. Can I stay here, or what?'

'S'pose. There are some stick mags under the bed if you wanna look at them. I'll see ya later.'

'Yeah, see ya.'

He disappeared. Not the smell though, that stayed.

Louis buzzed around for a while, and then stopped. I sat there for about half an hour. The stick mags had suspicious-looking stains all over them. Some of the pages were stuck together.

I had to get out. Then I had another brainwave. Of course. It was a Monday – the library was open. And it was absolutely the best place to hide. The old man never went anywhere near the library. Never.

Just as I was about to leave, Louis gave another buzz. I looked back. I realised I had the power – I could give that brave fly the gift of life.

I unscrewed the lid. Louis flew out of the mouth of the jar. He flew straight towards the window. Then he veered upwards, and slammed into the pane. He dropped to the floor. Dead.

Some gift.

The library was a little room at the back of the Institute. It had a musty smell, like the inside of an old suitcase. The librarian (volunteer of course) was Mrs Ashburner. She was reading a book. *Let Jesus be Part of your Life*, it was called.

'Hello, Mrs Ashburner,' I said.

She looked out over her tortoiseshell glasses.

Mrs Ashburner was the Sunday School teacher, the President of the Progress Association and the Country Women's Association, and the Secretary of the Save Our Institute Committee. A pillar of the community in other words. And that's exactly what she looked like – a pillar. Cylindrical, with hardly any neck.

'Hello, Tim,' she said in her sing-song voice.

'It's Gary,' I said.

She adjusted her glasses.

'So it is. All you Blacks look the same,' she said, smiling. 'Like peas in a pod.'

Mrs Ashburner knew very well who I was, but ever since I'd beaten her daughter Rosalie by a point to win the book prize at primary school, she'd called me Tim.

'Yes we do, don't we?' I said.

I started searching through the M&B section. I was looking for *A Circle of Opals*. Mum had returned it before I'd had a chance to finish it. I was dying to know what happened. Was the glamorous Mari really

247

up to no good? Was she desirous of the dark stranger Zac Heynes? Would poor Opal be denied the happiness that was rightly hers? Unfortunately it wasn't there. Maybe I'd never get to read it after all. For the rest of my life Opal, Mari and the dark stranger Zac Heynes would stay just as they were halfway down page sixty-three. Frozen in time, like those woolly mammoths they find buried deep in the ice. It was a terrible thought.

'I don't think that's appropriate reading material for a child your age,' said Mrs Ashburner, a frown on her face. 'The children's section is over there.'

'So it is. Thanks, Mrs Ashburner.'

I don't think the library had bought a new book that didn't have God or Jesus in the title since Mrs Ashburner had been librarian. Didn't worry me though. I took a Biggles from the shelf and sat on the floor.

'Did you want to borrow that?' said Mrs Ashburner.

There were no chairs in our library, you were supposed to borrow a book and then take it home. I suppose it was to stop old drunks like Reggy Porter from sitting there all day stinking the place out.

'I'm just seeing if I like it,' I said.

Actually I was really liking it. Biggles and Alfie were in a spot of bother over deepest, darkest Africa. But Mrs Ashburner kept bugging me.

'Have you made up your mind yet?' she said.

'Not yet,' I said.

'Well you'd better hurry. We're closing in five minutes.'

I'd forgotten, during the holidays the library was only open in the morning. I put the book back on the shelf.

'Thanks, Mrs Ashburner,' I said as I left.

'Not at all,' she said.

The old bag.

I walked back down the main street, trying not to look like Gary Black. The wind had got stronger, it was full of gritty dust. The bay was a mass of whitecaps. I could see a white station-wagon parked outside the pub. It looked like the old man's. I kept walking. It was the old man's. I peered in through the pub window. He was leaning on the bar, a glass of beer in his hand, talking to Ernie, the new publican. Ernie looked just like Big Mac; he had the same enormous gut. (Maybe Big Mac had left it behind.) But unlike Big Mac he went for the low option, belt looped below his gut, crotch hanging, trousers bunched up on his shoes. He sweated a lot too, did Ernie. But he didn't breathe heavy. Still, I reckon he'd get elected if he stood for president of the footy club. He had most of the right qualities.

The old man looked settled in for a day of serious drinking. There were some notes on the counter, a stack of coins on top. I was safe for a while.

Darcy was the only one on the jetty. He was fishing in front of the shed, sheltering from the wind. He seemed pretty happy to see me.

'Well gidday there, young'un, that wind's something ain't it?'

I agreed, the wind really was something. Then we

had quite a long conversation about maggots, which you probably don't want to hear. After that Darcy told a few yarns. Then I got him to recite 'Kaiser Bill'.

may you slip back through your arsehole
and break your fucking neck

The wind was like a gale now. It was impossible to fish so we ended up sitting in the shed. Darcy was teaching me how to tie a bowline.

'A bowline's the only knot you'll ever need to know young'un. You can do just about anything with a bowline.'

I wondered if a bowline could get the old man off my back.

'Who do you reckon wrote that up there?' I said, pointing to 'BOONGS PISS OFF'.

Darcy looked up.

'Crikey, young'un. I can't read that without me glasses. What's it say?'

'Boongs piss off.'

'Is that right. Well I dunno who wrote it.'

'They should do something about it, shouldn't they?' I said.

'I daresay they should, young'un. I daresay they should.'

I'm not sure if Darcy was making fun of me. There was a little smile on his face.

''Bout time to go, I reckon. You coming?'

'Sure,' I said.

We walked back down the jetty, leaning into the wind.

When I got home Sharon was in the kitchen. She was peeling spuds.

'Where's Mum?' I said.

'She's still in Adelaide. She rang just a while ago. She might have to stay there tonight.'

'Then who's looking after us?'

'The old man.'

'But he's down the pub.'

'What's new?' she said.

'What's for dinner then?'

'Mashed spud.'

'Is that all?'

'No, Mum said to get something from the butcher's. There's some money in the drawer.'

I went to open the drawer, then I stopped.

'Did Mum take her teeth with her?'

'Of course she did.'

'How do you know?'

'She wouldn't go all the way to Adelaide without her teeth.'

Good point, Shaz. I pulled the drawer open. No teeth, but some money.

I cycled back down to the main street, to the butcher's. Slogs was wearing a stripey apron; there was gunk all down the front of it. He had a newspaper spread over the counter, open at the form guide. He was scribbling all over it with a blunt pencil.

'Gidday,' I said.

'Gidday,' said Slogs. 'Whatta ya know?'

I never knew what to answer when people said this.

Well actually I know quite a few things. For instance, that the capital of Nepal is Kathmandu. Or the square of the hypotenuse of a right-angle triangle is equal to the sum of the squares of the other two sides. But I gave my usual answer.

'Not much.'

'Not much, eh,' said Slogs. 'Probably the best way to be.' He gave me a wink.

'What can I do you for, anyway?'

'Dunno. Something for tea.'

'Got sausages on special,' he said, pointing to a sign on the wall.

'SPECIAL THICK SAUSAGES $2.99 kg' it said. It was written in Texta; thick, black letters on a piece of butcher's paper.

'Yeah, they'll do. Give us a kilo,' I said.

As Slogs weighed the sausages I looked again at the sign. There was something about it, something familiar.

'Anything else I can get you today?'

'No, that's all thanks.'

He wrapped the sausages and handed me the parcel.

'There you go,' he said.

I gave him the money. He gave me the change.

'See ya round,' I said.

'Like a rissole,' said Slogs.

I opened the door to walk outside, but then I stopped and turned around.

'Forget something, did we?' said Slogs.

'I'm just thinking,' I said.

And I was, but not about meat. It was that sign, it

was bugging me. I looked at again. Then I realised. The 'S' was the same, a bit squashed, like somebody had sat on it. The rest of the writing, too. It was the same writing as 'BOONGS PISS OFF', exactly the same.

'No, that's all,' I said, closing the door quickly. I got back on my bike.

So it was him, Slogs, the transmogrified mettwurst, the 'Pleased to Meat You' man, he was the one. I should've known, he was such a creep. That night down the pub when Big Mac told that joke, it was Slogs who laughed the most; he laughed so much he spluttered beer all over the place.

And now I had him. Or did I? What could I do?

Tell the cops? There probably wasn't even a law against writing 'BOONGS PISS OFF' on the jetty shed. Except maybe defacing public property, but half the town (the male half) was guilty of that, including me. And even if he had broken the law, how could I prove it?

Your Honour, I'd like to draw your attention to the similarity in handwriting, especially the somewhat squashed nature of the letter 'S', between exhibit A – the 'SPECIAL THICK SAUSAGES' sign – and exhibit B – a photograph of the aforementioned 'BOONGS PISS OFF' graffiti. Based on this overwhelming evidence, Your Honour, I believe the accused, Mr Slogs here, must be given the maximum penalty that the law allows.

Yeah sure, Blacky.

Or I could confront Slogs. Tell him I knew he was

the one. And he'd probably say, 'So what.'

It was hopeless.

I passed Darcy's place. He was sitting on the verandah.

'Gidday, young'un,' he said.

'Gidday, Darce.'

Then it clicked. What Darcy had said earlier that day when I said they should paint over the graffiti – 'I daresay they should.' Now I understood what he meant. They should, but they couldn't because there was no *they*. Well, maybe there was but *they* were too busy. People were always at *them* to do things.

'They should really do something about that. They really should.'

They had no time, but I did. I had heaps of time. I couldn't tell the cops, I couldn't confront Slogs, but I could get rid of that stupid graffiti. And I could do it straightaway. Well, maybe not straightaway. After tea.

37

You'd think, wouldn't you, that with their parents away the Black tribe would run wild? But we didn't. Dinner was just like normal, maybe even quieter than normal. And it was delicious. The mashed spud was a triumph (well done, sis). The peas were okay. And the snags only tasted a little bit like mettwurst.

Team-man didn't say anything. He had a bruise on his face now, where the blood had been.

'Where you been today?' Chris asked him.

'What's it to you?' he said.

'I was just asking,' said Chris.

'Well, don't.'

He really was in a shit.

The phone rang. Sharon answered.

'Yes, Mum. No, Mum. No, he's not here. No, we'll

be fine. We will, Mum. Okay, Mum. Goodbye, Mum.'

I was thinking about the graffiti. How was I going to get rid it? I could scratch it out like I did with 'SHARON B GIVES HEAD', but that'd take ages. Or I could paint over it. But the paint was in the shed and the shed was locked and the old man had the keys and he was down the pub getting sloshed. I'd just have to wait until he got home.

After dinner we did the dishes, we watched telly, we brushed our teeth, we all went to bed at the right time. Who needs parents? I intended to stay awake, until the old man got home. So I lay there listening to the cicadas chirping, and I immediately fell asleep.

38

Slogsy is in his 'Pleased to Meat You' apron. And he really is a lump of mettwurst, fat and greasy. Two piggy eyes staring out. He's got a pen in his hand, one of those fat black Textas. He's scrawling 'BOONGS PISS OFF' everywhere. All over the shed. All over the jetty. In huge thick letters. All over the pub. The Institute. Everywhere you look. 'BOONGS PISS OFF. BOONGS PISS OFF. BOONGS PISS OFF.' Everywhere.

Me and Dumby are following him. I want to show Dumby something. And I keep saying, 'No, it's over here, Dumby Red. It's over here.'

But everywhere we go all we see is 'BOONGS PISS OFF'.

I'm getting more and more ashamed. My face is getting redder and redder, until flames are leaping from it. I spit on my palm and try to rub out the writing. It doesn't come off. In fact it gets bigger, darker. I start scratching at it. It still doesn't come off. But I keep going until my fingers are bleeding, until my fingernails are torn away.

Slogs is moving faster now. His arm is just a blur. Heading out of town. In all directions. Hundreds of Slogs scrawling away. 'BOONGS PISS OFF'. All over the peninsula.

I woke up sweating, my sheet tangled. Christ, what a dream! It was quiet, except for sound of the siblings breathing. Shadows across the walls. Through the window I could see the old man's car. I put on some shorts and tiptoed into the kitchen. But the keys weren't on the hook. I checked the car – they weren't there either. They were in his pocket.

39

The bedroom door was ajar. I got down on my hands and knees.

'Okay, let's go!'

Hands and knees didn't move. They were frozen. They were scared. We all were.

'Come on, let's go!'

Left hand twitched a bit.

'Come on, you can do it!'

Slowly, it moved forward.

'Yes!'

So did the right knee.

'Yes, yes, yes!'

Then the right hand, the left knee. We were away.

My nose pushed against the door. It opened wider.

The window was open, the curtains were parted. The room was full of moonlight. I could see him clearly, on the other side of the bed, under the white sheet. He was snoring.

I kept going, shuffling along the side of the bed, the smell of carpet shampoo in my nostrils. At the bottom of the bed I turned the corner, and stopped. I was starting to lose my nerve. In Mum's M&Bs, when the hero was in a situation like this, he'd take a deep breath. I took a deep breath. It didn't seem to help.

Then the moon sneaked behind a cloud and the room went black. My nerve returned. I turned the corner, the moon reappeared, but I had momentum now, I was heading down the main straight.

Two vicious-looking creatures with huge flappy tongues blocked my way. The old man's shoes. I pushed them under the bed.

I was there, right next to the old man's head. He was sleeping on his back, rumbling like a volcano ready to erupt. One arm was dangling over the edge of the bed. His overalls were hanging from the bedpost. I squeezed myself into the corner. My hand slowly slowly slowly crept into the pocket. There was something bulky – a wallet. I went deeper. I could feel them now, the jagged edges of the keys.

Then the old man mumbled something incomprehensible and rolled over onto his right side. The snoring stopped. But now his face was right next to mine. If he opened his eyes he'd be looking straight at me. I waited. I could almost see the blackheads on his nose. I could smell the beer on his breath. But nothing happened.

I grasped the keys tight so they wouldn't jangle and pulled them carefully from the pocket.

Then I gave the order. Hands and knees. Let's get the hell out of here!

Back down the side we flew, around the end, down the other side, through the door and into the corridor. My heart going thump! thump! thumpety thump!

But I had them, or I had it, the key to the old man's shed.

40

I unlocked the door, and rolled it up just enough so I could crawl under. It was dark inside, I couldn't see a thing. I had to turn the lights on. I flicked the switch. The fluoros buzzed, then burst into light.

The brushes were hanging up on a board. My old man loved painting. He was never happier than when he had a paintbrush in his hand. Or a roller. Actually he preferred a roller because then he could slap the paint on quicker. Still, he had a lot of brushes. And he really looked after them. It was probably because his old man had been a painter. He was brought up to respect them.

'A good brush'll last you a lifetime,' he'd say. 'And there's no better brush than a Carruther's Camel Hair.'

Actually the old man treated his Carruther's Camel Hairs better than he treated us. He'd spend ages cleaning them, making sure every single one of those camel hairs was spotless, much cleaner than when it was still attached to the camel.

He'd spiflicate me if he knew I took one of his brushes. What the hell, he was going to spiflicate me anyway. I took his favourite, the eight-inch.

Now the paint. There were tins and tins of it under the workbench. Any colour would do, I supposed, but when I pictured doing it in my mind, it was always with black paint. I kneeled down, and started sorting through the tins. Daffodil Yellow. Coral Sea Blue. Bushfire Red. Who made up these names? What was in their heads? Black Gloss. That's the one.

'What the hell are you doing in my shed?'

All I could see was two white feet, twisted and gnarled like mallee roots, under the garage door. Then the door rolled up with a screech.

The old man was in his underwear, white singlet tucked into y-fronts. His hair was sticking up. His eyes were bloodshot.

'Me?' I said meekly, looking up from the floor.

'Yes, you.'

Again, I decided to tell the truth. It was getting to be a bad habit.

'I was just borrowing some stuff. Didn't think you'd mind.'

'Borrowing some stuff?'

'Yeah, just a brush and some paint.'

'A brush and some paint?'

Did he have to keep repeating everything I said?

'That's right.'

'And tell me, why would you be borrowing a brush and some paint?' he said.

He sounded calm.

'Because I wanted to paint over some graffiti?'

'Some graffiti, eh? And where would this graffiti be, then?'

'It's down the jetty, on the shed.'

'And what does this graffiti say?'

I considered a slight deviation from the truth. I could say it said 'SHARON B GIVES HEAD' or, even better, 'BOB BLACK IS A BASTARD'. And all I was doing was protecting the good name of my father. No, that was too outlandish – I persevered with the truth.

'Boongs piss off.'

He scratched his cheek.

'So tell me if I've got this right or not. You sneak into my room and steal my keys. Then you sneak into my shed and steal my best brush and a tin of my paint. Why? Because you want to go down the jetty in the middle of the night and paint over a piece of graffiti that says "boongs piss off".'

I was surprised. He seemed to understand.

'That's right, Dad.'

'ARE YOU OUT OF YOUR FUCKING MIND?'

His lips were drawn back, like a rabbit caught in a trap. Little bits of spit flew from his mouth. The gold cap on his front tooth glinting, he took a step towards me. I scrambled back.

'What's happening?'

It was Team-man. He was wearing shorts, that was all. The noise had obviously woken him. Then the rest of the siblings appeared. First the boys. Then the three girls in their nighties.

'Back to bed, you kids,' said the old man.

They moved back a bit, then stopped.

'And you,' he said, jabbing his finger in the air. 'You can put those things back right now.'

Put the things back right now. Obviously that was the sensible option. Go to bed. Maybe he wouldn't even spiflicate me. Not yet anyway. The next day I could cycle down to Rocker's Garage, and buy a can of spray paint. Do the job with that. 'BOONGS PISS OFF' had been there for months, one more day wasn't going to make a helluva lot of difference.

I looked up at the old man. He was smiling now but it wasn't a happy smile. It was a mean smile, a my-son's-a-complete-moron-what-can-I-do-about-it smile. Behind him stood the siblings, all of them looking at me.

It was dead quiet, just the low buzz of the fluoro.

'I can't,' I said, softly.

'Eh?' said the old man.

'I can't put it back,' I said, louder this time.

The mean smile dropped off his face.

He turned around. 'Kids, did you hear what your idiot brother just said? He can't put it back.'

I got up. I was trembling. I took a couple of steps towards the door. The old man brought his arm back. I went to step past him.

Whack!

I went down. Like a sack of spuds. The brush flew out of my hand, the tin bounced off the concrete.

Greggy started crying. 'Daddy, don't hurt Gary,' he said.

I lay there, on the oily floor, looking at those twisted feet. My ear was stinging. There were stars in my head (and they weren't dead). Should I get up again? The spray can from Rocker's was starting to look like the better option after all. Maybe I just wasn't cut out to be a hero – my pain threshold was too low.

Then Claire yelled, 'The car!'

The feet moved away.

I got up. The car was rolling down the drive, slowly gathering momentum. Somebody was in the driver's seat. I could see the silhouette through the back window. It was Team-man! All the siblings were there except for him. And the keys were missing from the shed door.

'Stop, stop,' the old man yelled.

He started running after it. But he couldn't run, not properly, not with his soft feet on the sharp gravel. It looked like he'd just invented some weird new dance.

By the time he caught up the car was at the end of the drive.

He grabbed the door handle. It was locked. He started bashing on the window.

The car reached the main road. It didn't turn. It was headed towards the sea, straight for the cliff.

'The brake, the brake,' the old man was yelling, his hand still on the handle.

The car kept rolling. It just missed a post. The old man didn't. He collected it between his legs. He catapulted over and landed with a thud.

The car skidded to a stop, the front wheels an inch from the edge. Tim (formerly Team-man) hopped out.

(I stopped calling Team-man Team-man after that. Because he really was the first lemming (almost) over the cliff. The irony wasn't there any more. I mean you wouldn't call somebody Bluey if they really did have blue hair, would you?)

The other siblings arrived.

'Is he okay?' said Tim (formerly Team-man).

The old man lay there, on the road, in his underwear, not moving.

'I reckon he's dead,' I said. 'We've killed him.'

Then the light on Darcy's verandah came on. Darcy appeared. He was wearing shortie pyjamas with aeroplanes all over them. The pants came down to his knees. He had red slippers on, but no hat. I'd never seen him without a hat. His hair was grey and wispy.

'What the hell's going on out here?' he said. 'Helluva racket.'

'Somebody tried to steal our car,' said Tim (formerly Team-man).

'And Dad chased him,' said Sharon.

'He got hit,' I said.

'We think he's dead,' said Claire.

'Let's have a look here,' said Darcy, kneeling down next to the old man.

'Well, he's not dead,' he said. 'Looks like he got a knock on the head. And by the smell of him he's had a bit too much to drink. But he'll be fine. Maybe Doc Matthews should have a look at him in the morning.'

Thank God for that.

'Come on, you boys. We'll get him back up to the house.'

The old man moaned as we lifted him up. He weighed about a ton but we got him into bed. Then Darcy backed the car up the drive.

'Pretty smart thief that one,' said Darcy, as he handed Tim the keys. 'You kids better get to bed.'

'We will. Thanks Darcy.'

'Yeah, thanks a lot.'

I watched Darcy shuffling down the drive in his slippers. His light went out. I started walking towards the shed.

'Where you going?' said Claire.

'Down the jetty,' I said. 'Got something to do.'

'I might come with ya,' said Tim.

'Why not?' I said.

'I'm coming too,' said Sharon.

'So am I,' said Chris.

'Me too,' said siblings five, six and seven.

'I don't want to stay here all by myself,' said Greggy.

So in the end we all went, the eight of us, boys and girls, big ones and little ones, Brady Bunchers and Gilligan's Islanders.

41

We walked on the road. The air was still and warm. I could feel the day's heat seeping from the bitumen. There were no lights on in the houses. As we passed the caravan park, I could see a group of people, sitting in deckchairs, around a gas lamp. They were talking softly. (Probably about gents – mate, stick with the Darcy.) Nobody noticed us, barefoot and half-dressed, me with the Carruther's eight-inch Camel Hair in my hand, and Tim swinging a tin of Black Gloss paint, as we walked up to the jetty.

The jetty lights were off but the moon was big, almost full, and the sky was cloudless. Light sparkled across the bay.

We came to the shed.

'There it is,' I said, pointing.

'BOONGS PISS OFF'.

'What's a boong?' asked Greggy.

'A bad word for an Aborigine.'

'"Piss off" is a bad word too, isn't it?' he said.

'Sort of,' said Sharon.

'Why do they want the boongs to piss off?'

'Because they're racist,' said Tim.

'What's a racist?'

'Somebody who doesn't like Aborigines,' said Tim.

'Why don't they like the Aborigines?'

'Because they're racist.'

'Oh. Where will they go if they piss off?'

You know what little kids are like when they get going, question after question, like waves on the beach.

'Okay, enough questions,' I said. 'Let's get started. Open the tin.'

Tim took a coin from his pocket and prised the lid open. I dipped the Carruther's Camel Hair in. The paint was thick and sticky.

'I wanna go,' said Greggy.

So did Claire. And Kevin. And Chris. All the siblings did.

'Okay, a letter each then.'

'Littlest first.'

'Okay, littlest first.'

I gave the brush to Greggy. He climbed up onto the seat.

'I can't reach,' he said.

Tim hoisted him onto his shoulders. Greggy carefully painted over the B. Then he got down.

'I'm good at painting, aren't I?' he said, admiring his work.

'OONGS PISS OFF' it said.

Then it was Claire's turn.

'ONGS PISS OFF'.

Then Chris's.

'NGS PISS OFF'.

Then Kevin's.

'GS PISS OFF'.

Jenny's.

'S PISS OFF'.

Sharon's. (She did it very neatly.)

'PISS OFF'.

Mine.

'ISS OFF'.

Tim's.

'SS OFF'.

'Why don't you leave it like that?' said Chris 'It doesn't really say anything.'

'No,' I said. 'If a job's worth doing.'

'It's worth doing properly,' said Tim.

'You do the rest,' said Claire. 'It was your idea.'

'Yeah, go on,' said Tim.

I dipped the brush deep into the Black Gloss. Three swipes and it was gone. Not forever, but for tonight anyway.

The siblings started clapping and cheering, jumping up and down. Tim did his kookaburra. Claire stood on her head. Greggy did a somersault.

Gradually it became quiet again.

'What are we going to do now?' said Kevin.

The mood changed. The old man. None of us wanted to go home.

'We could sleep up here,' said Tim. 'It's not cold.'

'It stinks here,' said Sharon.

'What about Bum Rock, let's go down there,' I said.

'Where?' said the siblings.

'Black Rock.'

'Yeah, let's go to Black Rock.'

We walked back down the jetty. The lights in the caravan park had gone out. The whole town was dark, asleep. Instead of taking the road we walked along the beach, following the water's edge, where the sand was hard. Then we skipped across the rocks.

There was a little patch of sand next to Bum Rock. We lay down there, close together.

'Let's sing a song,' said Jenny.

She was big on singing, Jenny.

'What?'

But she'd already started, in that loud voice of hers, 'The Brady Bunch' theme song. Probably the most disgusting song ever written.

'You've got be joking!' I was about to say. But I stopped. I even joined in the chorus. 'The Brady Bunch. The Brady Bunch.'

Then we sang 'Gilligan's Island'. And a few other songs. There was silence for a while.

I looked up at the sky.

'Did you know,' I said, 'that some of those stars are actually dead?'

There was no reply.

I looked around. The erstwhile siblings were all asleep.

I closed my eyes. Tomorrow there'd be hell to pay, but at that moment, down there at Bum Rock, my brothers and sisters around me, I was happy.

Happier than a pig in mud.

I was as happy as Larry.

MORE YOUNG ADULT FICTION FROM PENGUIN

☆ ☆

Johnny Hart's Heroes   David Metzenthen

Working as first-time drovers for Johnny Hart, Lal and Ralph find themselves inching along a dusty, desperate road. There is a future there to be grabbed if only they can outlast the drought, roll with the punches, absorb the knockbacks, and stick together. But nothing is easy in the nineties in the not-so-lucky country. Especially when the odds are stacked, and not in your favour.

Winner of the 1996 NSW Premier's Literary Award (Children's books) and Honour Book, 1997 CBC Book of the Year Award for Older Readers.

Killing Aurora   Helen Barnes

Web is nine parts flesh, one part sulphur. And she's on a mission to save Aurora. But Aurora, the incredible shrinking girl, is already Death's best friend, and slips through Web's fingers like water. It's a bizarre love triangle, where there really are monsters under the bed. And not only can imaginary things hurt you, they can kill you. Volatile, original and blackly funny – *Killing Aurora* asks the question: does violence ever get you anywhere? The answer: well, sometimes . . .

Shortlisted for the older readers section in the 2000 CBC Book of the Year Awards and for the Ethel Turner Prize in the 2000 NSW Premier's Literary Awards.

Queen Kat, Carmel and St Jude Get a Life   Maureen McCarthy

A wonderfully passionate and absorbing novel about three very different girls in their first year out of school.

Shortlisted for the Victorian Premier's Literary Awards Shaeffer Pen Prize for Young Adult Fiction and the 1996 New South Wales State Literary Awards.

MORE YOUNG ADULT FICTION FROM PENGUIN

☆☆☆☆☆☆☆☆☆☆☆☆☆☆☆☆☆☆☆☆☆☆☆☆☆☆☆☆☆

Sleeping Dogs   Sonya Hartnett

The Willows are a dysfunctional family, and when one of the five children befriends an outsider who wants to uncover their secrets, the family's world is blown apart ... Another powerful and disturbing book from this talented young writer.

*Winner of the 1996 Miles Franklin Inaugural Kathleen Mitchell Award
Winner of the 1996 Victorian Premier's Literary Award Shaeffer Pen Prize.
Honour Book in the 1996 CBC Awards.*

Nukkin' Ya   Phillip Gwynne

Nukkin' Ya is the sequel to *Deadly, Unna?* Fifteen-year-old Gary Black, 'Blacky', isn't sure what he wants or where he is going. The one thing he does know is that he wants to escape the small country town he's grown up in, but for the moment, he's stuck.

Stony Heart Country   David Metzenthen

An insightful and beautifully crafted novel that explores the problems Aaron and his family face when they move to a small country town, where Aaron's father has to downsize the company that is the town's lifeblood.

Shortlisted for the Older Reader's section in the 2000 CBC Book of the Year Awards and for the Ethel Turner Prize in the 2000 NSW Premier's Literary Awards.

MORE YOUNG ADULT FICTION FROM PENGUIN

☆☆☆☆☆☆☆☆☆☆☆☆☆☆☆☆☆☆☆☆☆☆☆☆☆☆☆☆☆☆

Small Sacrifices Beverley MacDonald

Harry's family is mad and chaotic. But things really come to a head when they all have Christmas holidays in a dilapidated house by the beach. It's just as well Harry meets Angie. But as their relationship develops, Harry senses that there is a dark cloud hanging over Angie.

Eat Well and Stay Out of Jail Leonie Stevens

Vicky's looking to escape her life as head geek and loser of the year. She wants to travel, see the world and have a meaningful romance, so she visits her aunt in central Queensland. A kooky town, a mysterious boy, and a bunch of wackos hiding out in the scrub isn't exactly what Vicky has in mind when she dreams of taking to the road. But that's exactly what she gets. Will Vicky find the love of her life, or the end of her life?

Looking for Alibrandi Melina Marchetta

Josephine Alibrandi feels she has a lot to bear – the poor scholarship kid in a wealthy Catholic school, torn between two cultures, and born out of wedlock. This is her final year of school, the year of emancipation. A superb book.

Winner of the 1993 CBC Book of the Year Award for Older Readers.
Winner of the 1993 Kids' Own Australian Literary Award (KOALA).
Winner of the 1993 Variety Club Young People's Talking Book of the Year Award.
Winner of the 1993 Australian Multicultural Children's Literature Award.

MORE YOUNG ADULT FICTION FROM PENGUIN

☆☆☆☆☆☆☆☆☆☆☆☆☆☆☆☆☆☆☆☆☆☆☆☆☆☆☆☆

Vigil   Nadia Wheatley

Nathan's twenty-one, and he's running scared after the funerals of Tim and Dean, friends since primary school days. In search of answers, he returns to their home town, but the truth of the past, of their friendship, proves impossible to pin down. A gripping, complex fiction about the costs of searching for the truth, and the freedom it ultimately brings.

Thursday's Child   Sonya Hartnett

Harper and her family live in a ramshackle house in the country. Her brother, Tin, lives below them, building tunnels. It is the Depression and each of them is coping in their own way. One year their lives are changed forever by the misguided actions of a well-heeled neighbour . . .

48 Shades of Brown   Nick Earls

Dan's world is upside-down. He's living in a cool uni house but he's still at high school and his parents are supporting him. He understands calculus and 'The Simpsons', but the rules of friendship and love are harder to learn. Another brilliant, hilarious book from this hugely popular author.

Winner of the 2000 CBC Book of the Year for older readers

The Ivory Trail   Victor Kelleher

A gripping and magical journey between the past and the present linking five brilliantly realised past lives together. Follow the ivory trail yourself – be fascinated, be enlightened, and ask yourself, 'what have I discovered?'